OF

TOWERS

AND

ASSASSINS

KINGDOMS OF THE FAE

TIANI DAVIDS

To Alyssa. Remember when we all used to joke you'd be the perfect assassin?

To those told they're too much, and to those told they're not enough. To those searching, and those waiting to be found. He's waiting for you.

Books by Tiani Davids:

The Eldrasian Chronicles
The Dragon Healer
The Dragon Kin
The Dragon Queen

Kingdoms of the Fae
Of Swans and Princes (novella)
Of Glass and Cinders
Of Towers and Assassins

ELLCOMBE

KINGFORD

THE CONQUERED LANDS

DINAS CARDEN

EVERBREN

KILDUIN DESERT

FRIGARTH

LIGHTNING MOUNTAINS

JUNGLE

IDEN MOUNTAINS

EREAS FOREST

ASHENNOR

HYTHEMORE

N W E S

Eilah

T HERE'S NOTHING QUITE LIKE the thrill of the hunt. Finding tufts of fur, trails in the dirt, knowing you're getting closer to that final moment. The success of a kill ... Nothing tops a job well done.

But disappointment is sitting heavily in my stomach at the realisation that Lord Dennel of the Conquered Lands is not going to provide me with a good chase.

Lord Dennel is supposed to be in hiding, but the idiot has consistently had deliveries of food and wine sent into the forest every two weeks for months. It was a simple matter of following the cart here—barely a full day's walk from town—silently weaving my way among the trees and underbrush as it clattered along. Dennel may as well have walked himself into Ellcombe and saved me the trouble of following his near-worthless hide through this pitiful country. Then I wouldn't have to deal with the mess left behind.

There's nothing to learn from this job. Nothing that will make it easier for me when I can finally start the hunt I've been training for my entire life.

At least there's some money in it.

My bare foot slips on a patch of moss and I drop to one knee, mud soaking through my dark pants.

"Of course," I sigh, rising to my feet and jumping back onto the rocks I've been creeping along. I scan the ground in the light of dusk. The dip in the mud from my knee doesn't appear distinctly fae-made and could be from anything.

My first day out here had revealed that Lord Dennel and his men can't be bothered to scout the surroundings for a hunter. But it's best not to leave any sign I was here for the men who will come for the bodies. Whether it's Ellcombe or the Conquered Lands, better to be a wraith, a ghost in the wind.

I quickly cover up the depression and continue on, placing my feet slowly and softly, the ground cold. I'm too far away for Dennel and his men to pick up any sound if they're where they should be. But when does anything go exactly to plan?

A soft gust of wind caresses my skin, carrying the sweet scent of the decaying leaves and fresh earth. But it also sends my scent away from the cabin my quarry hides inside. Exactly as I want it.

Tonight is the night. There's no use waiting any longer. It's clear after four days of watching that Dennel's soldiers have a simple, unchanging rhythm. Two sentries patrol in the forest, one will be on the porch of the little hut, while one sits inside with the dear lord. The one inside naps during the day, but his being awake now means little to me. In fact, I grin. Four guards. Three fae and one human. Pitiful.

My stomach jumps in anticipation, and I rub my thumb along the thick ring on my finger and the dragon engraved there. This is all for her, and I'll make her proud.

When the dim shadow of the large pine tree I'd marked for cover on that first day scouting comes into view, I lower myself into a crouch and wait. A boot treads softly on the compacted earth, the faint crunch of dried leaves carrying to me. Three meters. Right on time. But I can't see him yet.

Another gust of wind, this time carrying the sour odour of sweat. I crinkle my nose. Lord Dennel can have food and wine sent out here, but apparently he can't make his men bathe in the river once in a while.

Two meters, and the fae finally appears. Crooked Nose prefers to patrol in his fae form, a sword in his hand while his eyes flicker off the path beneath his feet every four seconds.

More than enough time to cut him open.

My magic rises eagerly at my command, the icy daggers forming in my palms, crossguard and all. I smile at the familiar weight, watching as Crooked Nose passes my spot, oblivious to what awaits. I slink forward, light as the wind, and thrust my weapon through his heart.

A soft exhale passes through his lips, and I throw my weight against his before he can topple to the ground. I lower him onto a bed of pine needles, leaving my ice inside his flesh. The heat of his body and blood will have started melting it. It'll be long gone before anyone finds him.

I tighten my grip on the remaining dagger, siphoning my magic into it to keep it sharp and strong, ignoring the steel daggers at my waistline. Why use something so normal and easy to identify? I wish I could see the other lords' faces when they find the slightly rounded holes in these men that don't fit the description of any known weapon. It's part of the fun of the job.

My next target should be rounding the rear of the hut now. I creep through the scraggily underbrush in a large circle to come up behind him, watchful of the wind.

The back wall comes into view, log stacked upon log, the gaps filled with sap. There's another mistake Lord Dennel has made. He's sleeping in a human building, which means walls. And walls mean he can't see me coming. On second thought, maybe he chose it precisely for that reason. After all, it's not as if he's *tried* to remain hidden. I grin at the realisation.

Carefully lowering the branch that partially obscures my view, I watch the fox pacing the length of the wooden building in the moonlight. Unlike Crooked Nose, this fae patrols in his shifted form.

No way to sneak up on him. Good thing I've got excellent aim. Nearly as good as Mother.

Summoning another dagger into my free hand, I throw the first, then race after it on silent feet, my other dagger ready. But I needn't have worried. My weapon hits its mark, and the fox is thrown backwards, landing an inch from the wall, crimson blood shining on his red coat. Close. Too close.

I wait, an ear cocked.

Silence.

I'm almost disappointed.

Rule number one is not to take unnecessary risks.

Rule number two is to always have an escape plan.

And rule number three is nobody ever looks up.

I eye the roof of the cabin but shake my head.

Throwing caution to the wind, I put rule number one at risk. I could use a little fun tonight.

Straightening, I stroll around to the front of the cabin, casually walking into view of the guard reclined on the porch, his boots on the worn railing.

He jolts, jumping to his feet and squinting into the darkness. The only human on the guard team and they put him on the porch. They're practically asking me to kill him.

"Who goes there?" His voice is gruff. I'd bet this job's pay he's lowering it to sound intimidating. I stifle a chuckle and say nothing, watching.

The whites of his eyes show as he tries to find me. Dusk has passed, and the night may be dim for me and the other fae, but for him, it's now pitch black.

"Tilden?"

The young man draws his sword from his scabbard, still squinting into the darkness. His dark hair slides across his face and he shoves it back, searching furiously.

When the human raises his hand to knock his warning on the door, I throw my magic at him, forming the dagger even as I launch it.

It slams into his jugular, and he hits the decking with a loud thump. Grinning, I stride up the two steps to the door.

And knock.

Why have the human do something that I can do myself?

The tip of a crossbow bolt splinters through the door.

"Rude," I mutter, brushing wood chips from the chest of my black suit.

I take a deep breath, reaching into the stream of my magic, pulling it to the surface, whispering to it what I want it to do. Something exciting tonight, I think.

I kick open the door and throw out my hands.

"Wait!" a man shouts.

Ice darts shoot from my body, dozens and dozens of them spearing through the room, through the remaining guard still standing by the door trying to reload his crossbow, and through Lord Dennel still reclining on the couch, terror twisting his face. Wood splinters under the force of my ice, and blood splatters across the room, a drop landing on my face.

The guard's ruined body falls to the ground like a heavy sack.

In the silence that descends, I don't bother stopping to see if the two fae men are still alive. Their bodies are torn to shreds. Dramatic, I know, but Ellcombe wanted a message sent along with the deaths.

Consider this message delivered, I guess.

Turning on my heel, a headache forming, I disappear back into the forest. Maybe now, Mother will finally let me do what I was born to do; wipe the kingdom of Frigarth from the face of this earth.

2

Raiden

"I T'S TIME," I SAY, my gaze locking on the king and queen of Frigarth. Their eyes widen with understanding.

My queen exchanges a glance with King Turin across the small dining table, barely controlled hope shining in her green eyes. Turin's papers—spread across the stone table—are now forgotten, rustling in a soft breeze drifting through the open room.

"Are you sure, Raiden?" Laurel whispers, turning back to me. Grey has spread prematurely through her hair, grief and sorrow aging her faster than the years can pass. Any faster, and one might think she was a human, despite the delicate points of her ears.

I shake my head. "I've waited too long already. I never should have stopped searching."

"You never truly did," Turin says, his voice deep and rumbling. "We know that's why you asked to be an ambassador, Raiden."

Though the room is bright with the sun shining in with our lack of walls, and rebounding off the supporting pillars, it feels dark. Bleak. Matching our moods.

I nod, but the search for Princess Zara was harder than I expected it to be while dealing with foreign officials and their many, often petty, difficulties.

"There's been no sign of her. No whisper," I murmur.

Turin's voice tightens. "Where will you start?"

Not a day has gone by that I haven't thought about where I would go when given the chance. My answer comes instantly.

"With the assassins."

The king's eyes widen, and Laurel's face pales.

"Is that—" she stutters, "is that wise?"

I can see the way the memories pass before her eyes. The scars three separate attacks on her family have left behind, starting with the Dragon Assassin. They run as deep as the real scar I bear as a token of one of those attacks.

But it's the best place to begin. The assassins were there the day Zara was taken.

"The trail led me to the man," I say simply. "I never should have abandoned it."

Battle rages across her face, the same one that plays out every time I leave. The hope wins out each time, as it does now.

"You didn't abandon her, Raiden. You nearly died," Laurel says, quietly.

Turin reaches across the table to take her hand in his.

The king gives one sharp nod. "Please be careful, Raiden."

"I always am, Your Majesty."

"Will you stay for the rest of the day at least?" Laurel asks, trying and partially succeeding to throw off the sadness that weighs her shoulders down. "I want to hear about Cyra. Your message said there was trouble during your stay in Ashennor."

I smile at the memory of the queen's best friend and sister-in-law living in the nation to our south. "Cyra's well. She's been reunited with her human goddaughter."

The king and queen's eyes lighten for barely a moment.

"Really?" Laurel asks, tears of a different kind shining in her eyes.

"Indeed. It's quite a tale."

"Please," Turin gestures to an empty chair, "tell us everything."

"I'm glad you were there for Cyra," Laurel says, as I reach the end of my recount. "She is a strong woman, but your friendship in such a dark time would have meant the world to her."

"She is a force of nature."

Turin laughs softly. "That she is."

Laurel eyes me studiously.

"No one will replace your brother," I say, reading the searching look in her eyes. The question had begun to form there as soon as I spoke of the foreign princess—though she is our princess, too. It's a question Cyra's own nephew, Prince Jorai, appeared to have as well, though he never asked. I do not think Laurel would mind if Cyra and I had made that kind of connection, but the memory of her brother—Gaara—will always be with her. As it will always be with Cyra. "She is a good friend, but neither of us desires anything more."

"Straight to the point, as always," Turin says, a grin in his eyes. It's rare that a full smile manages to cross his face these days. The same can be said of his wife.

"It's always good to clear the air." I shrug. "I have already promised her another dance at Prince Jorai's wedding, too. I may have to request leave."

Laurel exaggerates a frown. "Then it's such a shame you'll already be going with us." Her frown clears, a grin tugging at her lips. "I suppose I can order you to dance with her instead."

"A truly dreadful duty." I bow my head, but catch the sparkle that enters her eyes. Job done. If I can bring either of them a single moment of joy, I consider the day a success. I wish I could bring them the one thing they truly need.

They both shift, sensing the change in my mood, and the heaviness returns like a blanket.

"When will you leave?" Turin asks, straightening his papers without a glance.

I hesitate. I would truly prefer to leave right now, and yet, something tells me my presence is needed for the rest of the day. "Tomorrow."

"Stop by before you go," he says. I've never left without seeing them, especially not on a trip to find their daughter.

"Always."

I spend the afternoon with my king and queen, joining them for a late lunch of mixed grains and vegetables topped with herbs from the east of the kingdom. A soft breeze plays across the room with the promise of sunshine and warmer weather.

The mood is light, but the shadow of Zara's loss never ceases to press upon us. I'm all that remains of the soldiers on duty the day she was taken. And the only one that knows the true depths of their pain. Laurel and Turin argue I don't deserve any punishment, the way the others did. Little do they know that being here is punishment itself. And punishment truly deserved.

Princess Zara's room remains untouched these seventeen years in a bid to preserve any possible information we might glean about what happened. I tread softly into the room, my bare feet silent and cold on the sparkling starlight floor. The water running underneath acting as a coolant.

The ghosts of that night cling to the room just as heavily as the dark stains of my blood on the floor. I shove the memories away and scan the darkness. Nothing new reveals itself, nothing has since the very night in question, but I can't stop myself from looking again. From hoping.

Zara was barely two when she was taken, old enough to remember snippets of her life if she tried, but young enough that her family would be strangers to her. The cot she slept in, decorated with the swirls of waves and waterfalls, the shelves with books and toys, the wide windows, and the crystal-clear floor made from crushed starlight with water running under it, would all seem the home of someone else.

I sigh, gazing through the windows. It's unusual for us to have walls, but even the fae can recognise they're needed when a princess becomes an active child learning to walk. They'd been installed to stop her wandering away, but instead, someone came and took her, escaping through them. Every single attacker our guards stopped or arrested were dead before we could question them. The rest escaped without a trace. Except for him. The assassin I'd tracked two years ago, the one I'll set out to find again in the morning.

"I thought I would find you here," Laurel's pained voice sounds behind me.

I turn, finding her eyes drifting over the room. Flickering light drifts in from the hall, but the main source of light is the luminescence of the starlight below us revealed at night. The flooring is transparent in the daylight.

"I'll find her."

Her eyes snap to mine, seeing deep inside me. "We never blamed you, Raiden. We're alive because of you."

I shake my head.

"You did everything you could."

"It wasn't enough." The words fall heavily from my mouth. Words I've repeated over and over inside.

"No," she whispers, her arms wrapping around herself. "But the fault isn't with you."

I swallow. "It doesn't lie with you, Your Majesty."

She crosses to the cot, her fingers trailing over the rails, her eyes fixed on the spot where her daughter had slept.

"I was—*am* her mother." Her eyes widen at the slip up and her hand flies to her mouth as a startled sob leaves her.

Dropping my hand to her shoulder, I give it a squeeze.

"Thank you," Laurel says, her voice breaking. "Thank you for never giving up on her."

"I'll bring her back." Whether she's still breathing, still walking this earth, or buried beneath it, I'll bring her back.

3

Eilah

I SNEAK INTO TOWN before dawn, wash the remaining blood from my skin, and am back in my creaking bed in the inn before anyone has peeked out of their windows or open homes. Staying in a human-based inn has its benefits. Like the solid walls surrounding my room that mean no one can see inside to know whether I'm there or not. This isn't the first time I've returned from a night out in the forest with no one knowing.

Growing up in the assassin compound certainly had its perks. Walls are a necessity in the Kilduin to block out the incessant sun and sand, and the hatred our kind shares of being enclosed is a weakness. A weakness I don't have. A weakness none of my brothers and sisters have.

I slip into the clothes of my cover—a travelling human woman on her way to see family, too poor for anyone to accompany her. I pull a blue dress over my head, long and loose flowing to hide my hardened muscles and countless scars. Boots cover my feet like a human. A thick ribboned necklace decorates my neck in place of my usual scarf, flush against my skin. My long brown hair is still braided back from last night, but I pull it free, letting it hide my ears and tumble down to the small of my back.

I turn my ring around, hiding the image of the dragon from prying eyes. There are some who might remember the symbol of my aunt or the tale of it if they're human.

Treading downstairs, I'm careful to make sure I don't avoid the third step that creaks on the way down to the tavern. I keep my expression unconcerned and vague as I study the room's occupants.

"There you are, lass!" Don, the innkeeper, calls from behind the bar. "I feared you had taken ill."

I glance outside, judging by the light streaking in, then look pointedly around the near empty room. Don's inn is the biggest in town, and I'm currently one of four patrons.

"It's still early."

He shrugs his massive shoulders. "You were up bouncing around at dawn yesterday."

"Traveling nerves," I say easily, pulling myself onto a wooden stool and smiling gently. "What's on the menu then, Don?"

"Porridge," the heavyset man grunts, his brown eyes flicking between me and the glass he's drying.

"Well, I'll take one."

"I'll get someone on it." He disappears through a door behind him for a moment before coming back to his place at the bar.

"What are your plans for today then?" He cocks his head. "Heard from your brother yet?"

I nod, smiling widely. To explain my stay at the inn—during which I couldn't guarantee how long I would be there due to my hunt—I'd told Don that I was waiting for my brother, who would accompany me on the remainder of my journey west. He thought that was very responsible of me, but that my brother should have come for me at my own home given "the times we live in." I promised him faithfully I would pass on the message.

"He's meeting me today on the edge of town."

"Ah." Don drops a mug of coffee on the bench for me. "I'll be sorry to see you go, but you tell that brother of yours he shouldn't keep a lady waiting so long."

I nod again, dutifully. My imaginary brother is certainly in trouble with Don, but the man's fatherly nature has been too easy to capitalize on. He even gave me my room at a discount.

A young human girl appears from the back room, a steaming bowl of porridge in her hands. Her curly brown hair sits low over her eyes and it's a wonder she doesn't trip over her feet. She looks nothing like her father, but Don says she's the spitting image of her mother. Blah, blah, I'd stopped listening somewhere around then.

"Thank you," I murmur, accepting the bowl. A few more minutes and I can shed this ridiculous, fake personality.

The girl smiles before hurrying back to the kitchen.

I gulp down the food with perhaps more gusto than a friendly, lowly human would, take a large mouthful of coffee, then stand to my feet.

"I'd better go, Don. My brother might be waiting for me."

"It was nice to meet you, lass," he says, running a hand through his thinning hair. "You travel safe now."

"I will."

Southlily is a small town by any standard, and yet it is one of the largest to have survived Ellcombe's attack on the country. There's a reason they call it the Conquered Lands, but this place has suffered the least, with the slowest introduction of new laws. Despite its size, Southlily is bustling with trade and travellers. But that only means that the town reeks of animal droppings, wet earth, and unwashed bodies. I fight the urge to hold my breath.

Waiting for a horse pulling a cart full of rotten apples to pass, I step out onto the dirt road lined with a hodgepodge of stone and wooden buildings. Careful to dodge the large piles of horse dung, I weave my way down the street, keeping my pace unhurried, though I wish it could be anything but. I can't wait to get out of this rotting town and onto a better job. Perhaps even the one I've been waiting for my whole life.

I need to get home to Mother.

But first, it's time to collect the rest of my payment.

Ducking off the main road and onto a narrow, cracked footpath, I slip into a poor dressmaker's shop. The little wooden store is empty of customers and will probably remain so for the rest of the day. The material is scratchy, the sewing uneven. Mother would have the owner whipped. But I'm not here for a dress.

"Is he here?" I ask the old woman behind the counter, a scrap of material and a bent needle in her hands. I let my eyes rake over her, taking in the leathery skin that hangs in bags from her jawline and arms, the too-thin frame, and the raggedy clothing. Wearing clothes that weren't akin to scraps would help her sell something once in a while.

She jerks her head, grunting as she gestures to the back.

I stride past her.

The back room is as dingy, dusty, and sparsely decorated as the front. Which is why my client is so out of place. In fact, I'd thought it odd the human had been allowed to keep his job at first. Lord Langford might claim to be working in the interests of the Conquered Lands, but a quick search of the home I'd followed him to after our last meeting revealed several letters from Ellcombe's officials stationed in these lands. One of which held the orders for the job I just completed. The idiot was yet to follow the instructions to burn the letter after reading it.

"Ah, Rebecca," Lord Langford says, turning from the smudged window that looks out over the little pathway.

My fingers twitch and the room's temperature drops. Fake name aside, I hate the way the word clings to the human's mouth. I'm just glad I don't have to hear him say my real one. Eilah would sound disgusting on his tongue.

He holds out his arms as though I might give him a hug, then thinks better of it and clasps his hands together. Langford's purple robe hangs from him, yards of fabric used in a vain attempt to hide his flabby body.

"It's done." I don't bother with any pleasantries. I have nothing to say to this sleazy traitor. I may not care what Ellcombe does, or any other country, as long as I'm free to kill who I want, but I can't stand a person that would betray their homeland. Too bad it seems they're the only people I deal with.

"Already?" His eyebrow raises.

"I'm efficient."

"That you are. Good girl."

I imagine wrapping my hands around his neck.

Lord Langford's lips curl under his thick, greasy, black moustache. Reaching inside the folds of his robe, he pulls out a small bag.

"Now that we've completed one transaction together, I don't suppose I could tempt you with another job?"

I eye the bag. "We haven't completed the transaction until I've been paid completely."

"Quite right," he says, throwing the bag.

I catch it easily, judging its weight.

"Can we talk now?" he drawls.

I suppress a sigh. I would much rather head home, but I'm already here. I may as well hear him out and get some extra coin.

I nod, tucking the bag inside my dress. I always have pockets sewn into my clothing, whether I make them or order them in. You can never have enough hiding places for a weapon. Or coin.

"I have a bit of an unusual job, but something tells me you'll enjoy it," he chuckles.

I raise an eyebrow. "I'm intrigued."

"I want you to kill Larson Kepler's infant son."

Raiden

I PICK UP THE trail right where I left it two years ago; in the grasslands outside of a small village north of the Iden Mountains. Any sign of our skirmish is now long gone, and returning to the site fails to prompt any new memories as I'd hoped. But I still make my eyes trail over the ground, remembering the way my men and I had fought the assassin I'd tracked for months. How we'd followed corpse after corpse marked with his signature as he'd headed south. The same mark I'd found on three of our dead guards in the palace after Zara had vanished so many years before. There'd been a young woman with him by the time we finally caught him.

I can still feel the way her ice-cold magic sliced into me. A nearly fatal blow. Goosebumps run along my skin at the ghost memory of the chill it brought.

Returning to the village fails to bring any more information to light. The people remember me and the fight. It was them who'd helped keep me alive long enough to get back to the healers of Frigarth. But they haven't seen the assassins since. Good news for them.

"Thank you," I say to the old soldier, a man I met here two years ago. His greying hair is thinning, his skin growing wrinkly. Humans wear age so differently, even among themselves.

"Sorry t' be of no 'elp, sir," he says, eyes drifting curiously to the swords strapped to my back.

I shake my head. "If you'd had news, it would have meant the assassins had returned and taken revenge on your people for their help. I'm glad that's not the case."

"Tha's true." He offers me a nod and turns on his heel.

I watch the man's retreating figure for a long moment. Sighing, I tear my eyes away and look south, seeing beyond the mountains. Perhaps I shouldn't have been so hasty about leaving Ashennor, not when they have rows and rows of records in the library. But I was anxious to return home.

Perhaps our southern ally has word of the male assassin. A man who marks all his victims isn't too hard to track, or at least his victims aren't. It would at least give me a place to start.

A small smile crosses my face. A quick stop is in order. I'm sure Jorai won't mind. And this time it won't be such a long journey. By air I can cut straight across the mountains.

I tug at the magic, raising it higher and higher, until I mould it over my body, concentrating on what I wish it to do. Bones and muscles shift and rearrange beneath shrinking and twisting skin.

In a moment, I am sitting on the stoned path in my shifted form; a rook. Launching into the air, I turn south, towards Ashennor and my friends.

Prince Jorai of Ashennor is out in the palace gardens. A sword is in his hand as he fights one of the soldiers who'd accompanied us in the rescue of the human slave Kaylin. Water and lightning swirls around them as they dart in and out, tapping their swords against each other, all with the backdrop of the starlight palace.

Squawking to draw their attention, I wait until Jorai has turned to face me and his lightning magic drops, before whipping past his face, batting his head with my wing.

"Raiden?"

I'm in my fae form within seconds, laughing as I cross the distance to the surprised Prince.

"What are you doing here?" he says, laughter in his voice as he grips my arm. He glances at the starlight palace. "Aunt Cyra and Kaylin are out. Are you staying long? They'd love to see you."

I shake my head as disappointment settles over me. "I was hoping I might use your library again? I need information on someone I'm tracking."

He nods, wiping sweat from his brow.

"I promised to help you with anything, Raiden." He turns back to the long-haired fae. "Sorry, Taavi, we'll have to pick this up again later."

"Of course, Your Highness. Raiden." He nods a bow, then hurries up the steps into an outer corridor of the palace.

"It's good to see you again," Jorai says, leading me inside, leaves crunch under our feet. "I didn't expect to see you back so soon."

"I didn't think I'd be back yet either, but if you have what I need, it could save me a lot of time."

"What do you need?" he says, turning his ice-blue eyes on me. He appears so similar to his father, and yet he never would have chased after Kaylin, a human slave.

"To find an assassin."

Jorai's head tilts. "An assassin?"

"He was there in the Frigarth palace, and again two years ago." We never discussed the particulars of what happened when Zara was taken nor in the attack that led to my ambassadorship, but I'm sure Jorai knows of it. The royal families of this continent can't keep much from each other.

His silent nod is enough to tell me I'm correct in my assumption.

"He leaves a mark on his victims," I say. "If he's been in Ashennor, you would have recorded it. It's a gruesome sight."

We turn into the library, the long rows of shelves packed full of worn books and tightly rolled scrolls opening up before us. I'd been here once on my visit to Ashennor, and yet the sight is surprisingly welcome.

Frowning thoughtfully, Jorai leads me over to a small shelf in the corner.

"Start here. I'll see if the librarian can help us find it faster."

"Thank you."

I pull down a book, its spine crisp and the ink still shining. Good. I take it to a nearby table.

I scan the pages, collections of suspicious deaths recorded in the country and surrounding areas listed in detail. There's not a lot of them, given the punishment is death or life in darkness, but born killers are hard to stop.

Jorai rounds the end of a shelf, his eyes landing on me. "It looks like we were in the right place," he says. "Which volume did you grab?"

I check the cover. "Two."

"He'll be in three." Jorai pulls the right book from the shelf and hands it to me.

I flip it open as he comes to peer over my shoulder.

The book is truly impressive, with some of the entries even including drawings of the crimes described. And that's how I know when I've found the right man.

Jorai shifts behind me, but he says nothing of the gruesome drawing detailing his signature.

I scan the page quickly and my stomach sinks.

"He's dead."

I read through the page again, slower this time. Kyler Thames was killed barely a month after my fight with him and his associate when soldiers from Ashennor caught him at the scene of an assassination.

"I'm sorry," Jorai says into the silence. "What will you do now?"

"The girl."

My best lead might be gone, but the young woman who was travelling with him might still be alive. She isn't mentioned in this entry. The thought has my stomach knotting, the ghost of her weapon sliding through my flesh again, but I shove it all aside. I need to find her.

I flip back through the book, finding the entries I'm searching for. They're not grouped together in the same way as the others, merely tacked in at the end of the book as open cases, small drawings detailing the deaths.

Weapon: unknown.

Except I know what she used. Because she used an ice dagger on me and my men two years ago. Grinning, I run a finger down the list, dismissing the ones that don't sound like her. There are gaps in the dates, which means she changes up her methods, but her ice magic is her favourite.

The last entry is for Ellcombe two months ago, and the image fits.

5

Eilah

IT TAKES LONGER THAN I'd wish to remove the blood from my dress. In the end I throw it out, changing into one of my darker dresses before stepping back out on the street. The old hag is right where I left her, and I can sense her eyes on me and my fresh dress, but she says nothing. I should have worn this one in the first place. Blood doesn't show up as easily on it. Maybe I should make that a subrule; always wear dark clothes in case of unexpected ... jobs.

Back on the main road, I've gone barely three steps when a quiet trilling draws my attention as a hawk flies over.

My stomach jumps and I cock my head. A message from Mother. Turning to follow the bird, I weave my way back up the street, narrowly avoiding being trampled by a large horse.

"Watch it, lass!" the rider yells, yanking on the reins.

"Sorry!" *Jerk.* One twitch of my fingers and that horse would slip on some ice and the man would find himself with a broken neck. But it would be a shame to hurt the horse. I force myself on.

The hawk disappeared over the forest to the north of Southlily, but nowhere near where Lord Dennel and his guards can be found. I wouldn't want to be discovered anywhere near the cabin. Rule number one—no unnecessary risks—counts even after the job is done.

I glance around, making sure no one is looking my way, and slip between the thick tree trunks. The bustle of the town is instantly dimmed, the air already cleaner, fresher. I sigh in relief. I can't wait to get out of this filthy town.

What could Mother want? I was planning on returning home anyway, but if this is a summons ... a thrill of excitement races through me and I pick up the pace, my steps silent despite my hurry. A lifetime of drills takes more than simple impatience to stop.

A break in the trees looms closer and when I push through, I find Nina waiting for me in her fae form. Her short hair is tied in a small bun on top of her head that's already pulling loose. She'll grow it longer soon, when it's time to move to the next stage.

"Sister!" She races over, throwing her arms around me.

I return the embrace, the sweet apple scent of her blonde hair filling my nose.

"It's been so long!" she says, pulling back. Nina might not be a real blood sister—I have none—but she is one of the few girls in the compound that the name truly applies to.

"I've been busy," I say, scanning her. Nina has always been smaller than me, in height and muscle build, but there is a slightly more defined air to her tanned form now. Even more visible as she's chosen to wear a close-fitting shirt and shorts. "You've been working hard."

She grins, jokingly flexing her biceps. "I wondered if you'd notice."

"How's training?"

"It's good," she says, bouncing on her toes. "Really good. I think I might be allowed a job soon. A proper job."

I nod. Despite being in the compound almost as long as I have, Nina has never completed a paid job from a client. Sure, she's killed in training, but she's never been out there on her own. Instead, she's been stuck on messenger duty with the shame of having shorter hair than most. Mother thought she was better suited to it and I'd have to agree. So there's just one problem.

"Who'll replace you? You've the swiftest form of us all."

Mother's most important messages depend on her.

"No one." Nina frowns. "Mother wants me to keep delivering for her. I'll be able to do jobs around them."

I purse my lips, looking her over again. With no other magic, she doesn't have an edge in combat. Well, any more of an edge than others without magic. Mother is right not to replace her, even if it's not what Nina wants. It's our talents that define us.

"A good balance," I finally say. "Do you have a letter for me?"

"Yes. Two actually." Reaching into her back pocket, Nina pulls out the crumpled notes and hands them to me.

Unfolding the first, I scan the coded message written in Mother's elegant slant.

Nina waits all of two seconds before asking me, "What does it say?"

I let a smile cross my face for Nina, though frustration threatens to wipe it away. I'd much rather be heading home. "I'm going to a party."

Another job from Ellcombe in the Conquered Lands. They must be planning something. Shrugging, I open the other note.

And my heart drops.

"Eilah?"

That can't be right. I read it again in case I used the wrong code.

"Eilah?" Nina demands.

I don't look up.

"It's—it's a job in the north. Another lord."

It's not.

The target is one of my sisters planning to leave the continent. Aeris. She should have known Mother wouldn't let her leave. She should have known I'd be the one sent after her. Mother might not know where Aeris will go, but I do. Of course I do, because I was the one sister she bared her thoughts too. Stupid, stupid girl.

But to let Aeris believe she might actually escape, only to snatch it away at the last moment ...

"Can I come?"

"No," I snap. Closing my eyes, I inhale deeply. "No. I'm sure Mother has more messages for you to deliver."

"Fine," Nina grumbles, crossing her arms. "Come home when you're done. It's boring without you."

"I will."

Her body gives one large shake, and she stands before me in her hawk form, ruffling her feathers. With a gentle trill, she shoots into the air, heading south. Leaving me standing in the clearing, wishing I could follow her home. Wishing someone else could take that second job from me.

Despite the sun, a shiver traces down my spine.

How could Aeris be so stupid?

As of Mother's letter, she hadn't left yet. Which means I have plenty of time before Aeris gets to the coast, weeks even. I count on her first few days being slow going.

... How did Mother realize she's going to leave?

Sunlight flickers over the ground and a gentle wind caresses my face, but a restless energy settles over me in its wake. The kind I haven't felt in a while. The kind that will be dangerous in my upcoming missions. I need to get this out of me. I need a fight.

And I know exactly where to go.

I bury the letters in the earth, and turn back towards Southlily. I'll need a horse.

6

Raiden

I SKIRT THE EDGE of Ellcombe, listening for any whispers in the outer towns of unusual or mysterious deaths. It would be foolish to go into the heart of the enemy's territory, but if it means finding Zara, I'll do it. Though Ellcombe has long denied any involvement in the princess's disappearance, I wouldn't be surprised if they had hired the assassins. It's no coincidence that an assassin killed Prince Gaara, and others took Princess Zara, his niece. But the Dragon Assassin is dead, and so is the man I'd set out to track. This girl better be able to tell me more.

The closer I draw to Ellcombe's capital, Kingford, the more whispers I hear. I'm dangerously close, but my rook form allows me to get closer than I would dare as a man. But it's not a job in Ellcombe that the fae and their human slaves speak of. It's a mass killing in the Conquered Lands. A lord wanted dead for inciting rebellion against Ellcombe was found torn to pieces, his guards slain with a peculiar weapon, and no one knows who did it. But they are all excited.

Lifting my left wing to the wind, I turn, following the whispers.

They lead me to the second largest town in the Conquered Lands. Southlilly.

"It's all quite a mystery," Lord Langford says, wincing as he reclines in his high-backed chair. The lord was the first person I sought out upon arriving in this small town barely holding on to its roots. All the important messages pass through him—on Ellcombe's orders. "I've seen the bodies, and I can tell you I've never seen anything like it."

"I need to see the bodies myself, and the site of the killings," I say, letting my eyes run over the lord. His long blue robes hide much of his large form, but they don't hide his injury as effectively as he hopes. His shoulder. That's what's troubling him. If it wasn't clear this man has never gotten his hands dirty in his human life, I might suspect he'd gotten it killing Lord Dennel himself. And that would also mean that Lord Langford is acting on less official orders from Ellcombe, ones that would dismantle what little independence his own country still has.

He shifts, wincing again and sweat beads on his forehead.

"Of course. Justin can take you out there," he says, referring to the boy who'd let me inside the lord's large home. It's one of the few completely stoned buildings in the town, and certainly the biggest. How the human has managed to retain it while under Ellcombe's rule must be an ... interesting tale. "As for the bodies, they're at the healer's."

"Thank you."

Lord Langford nods, sweat rolling down his forehead. He's clearly struggling to maintain his composure with that wound. "If that's all, I have work to do."

"I'll see myself out." I turn, keeping my eyes from scanning him again. If what my gut is telling me is true, I can't have him wondering what I might know.

But I'll be back once I see the bodies.

There is no sign of whoever killed Lord Dennel in the forest. No footprints. No broken branches. Nothing out of place.

Whoever it was, they travelled a long way without leaving even a blade of grass bent. My neck prickles, a question, an idea waking.

"What is it?" Justin stands beside me, his dark eyes scanning the forest. The young human jumps at every little noise. Can't blame him if what the whispers are saying is true.

"Nothing," I say, straightening. "They're very good."

The boy tugs at his shirt collar, a bead of sweat tracing down the side of his smooth face. He's barely hit puberty.

"And long gone."

"Right," he murmurs, his eyes still jerkily searching the forest. "Long gone. Are you sure you don't need those swords, sir?"

"Wait here." I leave him in the trees outside of the cabin, leaving my swords in place at my hip. He doesn't need to see what's inside. I can smell it from here.

There is blood on the wall to the left of the door, dark on the rough wood. It splattered on the wall, but the blood on the decking has pooled. Stepping through the entry reveals a scene more gruesome than the ones on the porch and in the forest.

Torn to shreds.

The room has been torn to shreds. Ripped apart. As though hundreds of arrows had shot through the room at a speed impossible for a bow to produce.

There is more than blood on the floor and walls.

I swallow heavily.

Magic. Powerful, bold magic.

Pivoting on my heel, I retrace my steps, finding the human boy right where I left him.

"Take me to the healer."

"I'd certainly be grateful for any help you can offer. It's got us all quite perplexed. I wouldn't be surprised if magic were involved, sir, but what kind of magic can rip someone to shreds?" The doctor leans over what's left of Lord Dennel, crinkling his nose, brow furrowed.

"You've seen the cabin?" I raise my eyebrow.

He straightens, running a handkerchief over his face. "Yes, I was one of the first to see it, sir."

I can't say that the wounds on Lord Dennel and the guard found with him match what I would expect of the assassin and her daggers of ice. But the thought lingers.

"Can I see the others?"

"Of course," the doctor says, leading me across the room. Tugging a white sheet back, he reveals the body of a strong fae male. "The wound is in his back, straight into the aorta. Quite efficient."

"May I?" I gesture at the body. I need to see it.

He nods, watching curiously as I lift the man's stiff form.

Yes. This is what I was expecting. A jagged edge, more rounded than a normal dagger.

"Have you seen this before?"

"No," I murmur. Returning the body to his back again. My wound is something different, and yet clearly from the same type of weapon. Inflicted by the same woman.

A woman even more powerful than I suspected.

"I assume whoever they are, they won't still be here? Unless they're after Langford too." The man pats at his damp face again.

"Langford is quite safe." And not only because this assassin is gone. "The objective was to stop the rebellion. Dennel's plans have died with him."

"He was a fool," the healer says, shaking his head. "There's not enough of us left to fight Ellcombe."

"It would be easier if so many of your people weren't helping them."

But Ellcombe's presence will only grow now.

It's time to speak to Langford again and learn about the woman he hired. And why she stabbed him in the shoulder.

7

Eilah

Dinas Carden is completely different from Southlily. Once the capital of the old country, it has been reshaped in the Conquered Lands to suit Ellcombe's growing presence. Ellcombian soldiers patrol every block, follow every official, and enforce the new anti-human laws of the land. I won't find any human owned inns here, but the new lords haven't finished knocking down the enclosed buildings and it's still possible to find a dash of fun if you know where to look.

I dismount the grey mare at the city gates as the first streaks of dusk cross the sky, tossing a coin to the stableboy. The party Mother wants me to attend isn't for three more days. Which leaves two for reconnaissance, and one for fun. I'm starting with the fun. I deserve it.

Pulling my scarf up to cover my nose and slinging my bag over my back, I disappear into the winding city streets. A conquered city is always changing its face, but the bones remain the same, and I find the Fire Dragon easily. I heard it was one of the first human-designed buildings to be converted to the open plan of the fae. There are no walls, merely columns and a roof overhead. Just the way the fae want it. I would have preferred a dark corner to disappear in, but I'll take what I can get.

The tavern is filling up fast, but I find a seat and wave to the barmaid for a glass of loi. I can't afford to drink anything else, not when it would compromise my senses. This place makes my favourite drink from the sweet yet tangy berry, anyway.

"Hear about that lord over in Southlily?" a large fae man says loudly from the bar. His black hair rivals mine for length, but he clearly doesn't know, or care, how to look after it.

His friend nods over his mug. "Who hasn't, eh? Torn to shreds, they say."

A satisfied smirk crosses my face. Message definitely delivered.

"Serves the fool right," the first man says. "Fancy thinking you could stop Queen Karas herself. The lady won't even forgive her daughter!"

The second man stiffens, glancing around nervously at the mention of the Ellcombian ruler and her heir. The two soldiers at the table across the room remain oblivious, too taken with their drinks and women to hear.

"Shh!" he hisses. "Don't mention the girl!"

"Here you are, ma'am," the barmaid says, placing a glass of golden liquid on my table. Her face is set in a permanent frown, wisps of hair escaping from her bun.

I shoo her away, reclining in my chair and pretending to examine a painting on the nearest pillar to hide my true interest; the two fae men who have had slightly too much to drink. Which is hard because the painting is truly beautiful despite its lack of a clear subject. I especially love the red and silver mixing together. Finn must be bringing in a lot of money to afford these.

"All I'm saying is, Lord Dennel was an idiot," Long hair says.

On that, we can agree. I take a distracted sip of my drink. It fizzes on the way down. Not bad.

"That he was," the other man grunts.

But my sources of information are done gossiping for the night. They slide two gold coins across the smooth bar and push their chairs back noisily.

Unhelpful.

The barman, a thin, sickly looking man with dark eyes and grimy blond hair, snatches the coins from the wood and tucks them away in his apron pocket. I cock my head. A human. And certainly not the owner.

I scan the room, not turning my head too far to avoid being obvious. But Finn isn't here tonight. He's certainly not working. Looks as if he has a good thing going for him. Either that, or the fights have started earlier than usual.

Fae hearing extends far, and most in the bar would be able to hear anything said in the room if they tried, but I'm the only one here not searching for distraction in a bottle. I jump between several conversations, sifting through the rush of the fire in the centre of the bar, the drunken laughter, the slap of mugs on tables, searching for any scrap of news about the fight. The Fire Dragon can always be counted on for the juiciest of gossip. And nothing tops a fight.

"We're going to be late," a woman on the next table over whispers to her friend, glancing out into the gathering dark.

"Finn said two hours after dark," the small and thin woman says dismissively.

The woman shakes her head, revealing a thick scar on her bare, strong shoulders. A fighter. I resist the urge to sit up a little straighter.

"He always starts early."

The small woman takes a last gulp of ale and stands, a vicious smile on her face. "We'd better go then."

I wait until they're on the street before slipping from my table and strolling out after them.

The key to following someone is confidence. If you appear to belong, no one questions a thing. The streets are crowded tonight, and the two women are an easy mark. I simply keep four meters behind, stop now and then to glance inside a shop, and they lead me to the Starlight Club on the other side of the city.

I snort.

The entire building is coated in a layer of crushed starlight, making it shine silver in the night. And Finn chose this place for an underground fight. How ... like him.

Fast-paced string music rises from inside, the beat so loud it vibrates in my chest. I can't see the musicians over the bodies packed together, jumping and swaying in time with the beat. The fight won't be on this main level. No, there must be a room below.

A dark, enclosed, stuffy room that the other fae will hate. A wriggle of dissatisfaction creeps in. This could be an easy night. But then ... perhaps the other fighters will have been here before.

Shrugging, I push my way into the dancers, keeping an eye on the two women I followed. The bodies reek, a mix of sweat and too-strong perfumes. A soldier bumps into me.

"Apologies, miss," he says over his shoulder, continuing on his way.

Huh. I wonder if the man is aware of the fights happening below. But being right under the law's nose is half the fun for Finn. Even better in his books if soldiers join in.

The women slip behind the musicians to where a fae man stands beside a thick silver curtain. He could be a bodyguard scanning the crowd if I didn't know better. He looks the women over, nods, and they slip through the curtain. I wait a moment, then sidle over, tugging my scarf down from my face.

"Is Finn in?" I ask, keeping my voice low.

The man cocks his head, a strand of hair escaping his loose bun. A large jewel hangs from his earlobe. "Who's asking?"

"An old friend. We've partied before."

His blue eyes scan me, head to toe and then once again, taking in the daggers now strapped to my thighs. It's not an uncommon look, but this time the man seems to get the true measure of me.

"I'm sure you have."

He tugs the curtain aside.

And reveals a small room, curtained off from the street.

"Another one?" a young fae male says, glaring from a table he and three others appear to be playing a card game at.

I nod.

"Hurry up then," he sighs. "We only just started playing again."

He stands, pushing his chair aside and lifting a rug from the floor, revealing a wooden door barely wide enough for the bodyguard to slip through.

He tugs it up and I glance down. Three meters. I climb down the rickety ladder and the door closes above me, leaving me in shadow. Rule number two—always have an escape plan—isn't looking so good, but then, this isn't a job and I've been in worse places.

"Fightin' or watchin'?"

"Bit of both." I don't bother glancing at the source of the voice, my eyes already locked on the fight happening at the end of the hallway. But I can barely get a glimpse of it through the large crowd.

"Head on through to register. Got a few ladies tonight."

I turn a feral grin on the man standing watch over the trap door.

"Oh, I'm not a lady."

He returns it. "My mistake."

Flames light the way, set in brackets in the middle and at the end of the hall, more for dramatic effect than any real need among the fae. But then the room opens up and the torches line a stoned space as large as the club above us. Oh, Finn chose a good spot.

There are two fights happening, with fae crowded around both in a large circle. Screams of encouragement and jeers echo through the space.

I search the large crowd for Finn.

"Eilah? Eilah! It is you!"

I swing around to find Finn has found me first. He always was good at spotting a fighter.

In his fighting leathers, Finn pushes through the crowd, his blond hair cropped shorter than the last I saw him. A new scar decorates his left biceps, but otherwise, he appears healthy. He must be at least two hundred, old enough to be my father, but that doesn't stop his eyes from sparkling as they lock on mine.

"I thought something or someone had finally caught up with you. Where have you been?" he says, crossing his arms as he stops in front of me.

"Busy," I say, smiling. He's a sucker for a good smile.

"Please tell me you're here for a fight?" He rubs his hands together.

I nod, glancing at the closest fighting pair right as one of the men lands a spinning kick to the other's jaw.

"And please tell me you have some good fighters."

His smile widens, revealing perfectly straight and shining teeth. "Only the best for you."

"I appreciate it, Finn."

He steps closer. When he leans in, the scented oil coating his skin bites at my nose. "One day you'll have to tell me where you learnt it all."

I laugh. "Oh, I don't think so."

"I don't suppose you'd be interested in fighting in your shifted form? We have fights dedicated to them now." His eyes run over me, as though picturing it.

"Really?" I raise my eyebrows. It's tempting, I'll admit. But I don't relish the taste of blood in my mouth or the flesh that gets caught in my canines. "I think I'll stick to this form."

"It is a good one," he says, grinning.

My fingers twitch.

He continues, oblivious, "How about the next one, then? No magic. First to draw blood wins. The usual."

"How much?" I'm not a fool. Finn stands to make a decent amount on my fight, and I may as well get my share.

"For you, darling? A quarter."

I shake my head. "You and I both know how much I'm about to make you, especially if you do your usual trick of making them think I'm nobody. I want half."

The light leaves his brown eyes for a moment, but then he laughs. "You always could strike a bargain. Consider it a deal, sweet Eilah."

"Good."

He claps his hands. "Follow me."

Finn leads me through the bustling crowd to the head of the room. I study him from behind. He's been fighting tonight. That much is clear from the blood on his leathers.

He might think highly of his skills, but he wouldn't last in a real fight down here. Someone must have rigged one for him. I'd rather enjoy jumping in the ring and teaching him a thing or two about bloodshed and how to talk to a woman.

Especially one that could kill him in thirty-two different ways with her bare hands.

"Poppi," Finn calls as we near a human with a notebook clutched in her hands. The girl, not much younger than me, looks up with round eyes. I don't miss the shackles between her ankles.

I miss a step, but Finn is too occupied with the slave girl to notice. Of all the low and disgusting things I knew Finn to be and do, I never thought he'd keep a slave. But I keep my face blank, a perfect mask as I gaze into the barely controlled terror shining in her eyes.

"Put Eilah here down for us, will you? She'll fight next."

"Yes, sir." Her voice is surprisingly steady.

I could free her with my winnings.

I shove the absurd thought aside. Doing so would put me in a bad place with Finn and every Ellcombe-lover here. No. I might be taking a small risk here tonight, but I'm not throwing rule number one out completely. Not for anyone or anything.

I don't bother asking who I'm fighting. That's not how it works down here. You don't know your opponent until you step into the ring. Adds to the challenge.

I shake the energy from my hands. Aeris is still on my mind. That stupid, reckless—

"Nervous, Eilah?"

I shoot Finn a withering glare, but I don't miss the way his eyes narrow. "Loosening up, Finn. When have I ever been nervous?"

He raises his eyebrows and his hands. "Just making sure you're not going soft on me, pet."

Eww.

But snapping will make him think me more nervous. Instead, I cock my head.

"Get me in the ring."

Laughing, he slaps me on the back.

I grit my teeth. I swear this man wasn't this annoying the last time I saw him.

"Any second now, judging from *that*." His lip curls.

That is a fae man crawling across the floor. Actually *crawling* away from his attacker.

"I hope you didn't bet on him, Finn."

His face darkens. "Not at all. I know talent when I see it."

His gaze shoots to me. "And you are it."

I nod. Good. He'll bet high on me thanks to the display of cowardice playing out before us. It couldn't be better timed.

With a loud roar, the crawling man's opponent kicks him in the ribs, flipping him over, and slams his fist into his brow.

Blood spurts.

The crowd jeers as the loser is dragged away. Pathetic.

Finn throws me a rogue grin and pushes his way into the ring.

"Ladies and gentleman, give it up for Dacian!"

I stand silent as the onlookers cheer, as though the men had given them a good fight. Honestly, Poppi could have done all of that. And that's saying something considering the girl's feet are tied together.

"Next up, we have a returning champion and a new challenger!"

I wonder which one I am tonight.

"Please welcome Rezie!"

Judging by the crowd's excitement, I'd say she's the champion and I'm a new face tonight.

The woman I'd followed here from the Fire Dragon pushes through the spectators, clad head to toe in a close-fitting, black uniform. I take the moment to study her. She carries herself well, with the sword at her hip looking as natural as an arm or a leg. Her eyes are clear despite the stop at the tavern, and her hair is shaved short. My eyes lock on her ears. Earrings. Long, dangly, grabbable earrings.

Too easy.

"And the challenger tonight," Finn yells over the crowd, "is Rebecca!"

I force my step to hesitate, the grin not to show as I enter the ring and pull my scarf over my nose again. My eyes lock on Rezie for a moment, and then I look away. The picture of a girl in over her head.

No one said I have to fight fair. In fact, I'm merely playing Finn's game. Rebecca actually fought for him before, but no one will remember that meek little girl who fought in a lower level for an easy win and even easier money.

But they'll remember tonight.

Finn is telling me he wants a show by using that name. And a show he'll get.

The ground is stone. Slippery with blood already, but my rough feet grip the ground easily.

"The rules: first to draw blood wins. No magic. And, ladies and gentleman, this time our fighters are using weapons."

I force my eyes to widen, glance around as though I've made a terrible mistake as the crowd screams in approval.

Rezie smirks. "I think you might be in the wrong place, girl."

"Fighters, get ready!" Finn steps out of the way, and Rezie draws her blade.

I pull my daggers, make my hands shake slightly, and lock my eyes on Rezie.

"Begin!"

Rezie lunges.

I jump back, not even raising my daggers as her sword swings past me. She follows through with a side kick and I step back only enough that her boot grazes my side.

The spectators roar, and I can imagine Finn's smug face as the bets are placed against me.

I know how to work a crowd, and this one is the same as any other.

Rezie steps back and there's a gap noticeable enough that not to go for it would be foolish. So I jump forwards, but bring a dagger up slow enough that the fae woman blocks it easily. My other hand twitches and she pushes my blade away and whirls behind me. I duck instinctively and her sword passes harmlessly overhead.

Still low, I sling my leg out and spin around to sweep her legs out from under her. Rezie's eyes widen and she barely manages to jump, sliding in a drop of blood.

We step back from each other, weapons held ready.

"An actor," Rezie purrs, her eyes narrowing. "Stop pretending to be a meek child, Rebecca. I could see that mind working from the moment you stepped in the ring."

I shrug. "It was simply too much fun. I can't stand a fight that's over too quickly."

"On that, we can agree." She lunges, but I'm ready.

The crowd fades into the distance as Rezie and I enter the true fight, whirling, slashing, stabbing, back and forth, and on and on. She's good. But I'm still holding back. Still keeping myself from revealing just how good I truly am. Because I can't have anyone asking questions. But this is the best fight I've had in these pits, and I let it play out a little longer. Let her tire.

Her earrings flash past and I almost pull on them, almost end the battle there with the ruination of her flesh. But instead, I drop my blade and let it slash the back of her hand. Call it womanly admiration, but I couldn't send such a skilled fighter home with a hole through her ear that would never heal. I'm not that heartless.

The crowd roars. Screams. Jeers. And cheers.

Rezie smirks as she steps back, the blood dripping from her hand, and nods.

Before Finn can enter the ring again, I cross the space to her, all thought of fighting gone.

"Next time," I say, "don't wear the earrings. They were all too tempting to pull."

"I'll remember that," she says, puffing, fingering the jewels.

"And the winner is: Rebecca!" Finn yells, stopping beside us. The crowd grows even louder.

He turns to me, lowering his voice as Rezie leaves. "Well done. Wait for me to call the next fight and you'll get your winnings."

8

Raiden

"Ah, you're back," Lord Langford says, closing the doors behind him on the meeting I've interrupted. He has the presence of mind not to let his annoyance show.

"Indeed." I keep my voice emotionless, my face blank, all friendliness and civility gone.

His steps hesitate almost imperceptibly, but when he speaks, his voice is steady.

"What did you find?"

The lord's arm sits stiffly at his side, his hand tucked into a deep pocket in his robe to keep it from moving. I let my gaze linger on it.

"Let's talk in your office."

"Yes. Of course, this is hardly the place." He swallows heavily.

I gesture for him to lead the way, following closely behind the traitorous lord. Water trails down the back of his hairy neck.

It's a short walk down the luxurious hall to Lord Langford's office, where I met with him yesterday. The room is large, decorated with banners and rugs and portraits. He's spent his money freely. Blood money, no doubt.

I close the heavy doors behind us as Langford strides towards his large, ornate chair.

"How much did you pay her?" I say softly.

This time he stumbles in his steps, gaping over his shoulder. "Excuse me?"

"How much," I say, striding towards him, "did you pay the assassin?"

"I—that's not—" His face reddens. Langford takes a deep breath, thrusting back his shoulders. "How dare you accuse me of such a thing!"

"Relax," I say, sitting heavily in the high-back chair behind his desk. I lean back, setting my feet on the papers strewn across the wooden surface. "I'm merely curious."

A bitter taste enters my mouth at the farce I'm entering, but there's particular information I'm after, and Langford won't give it if he thinks I'm a soldier here to arrest him.

The lord cocks his head, his beady eyes running over me. He glances between his chair that I'm sitting in, and the one usually reserved for guests. He sits in it.

"You're from Hera, aren't you?"

I hope he doesn't notice the pause that barely lasts a heartbeat. "Yes."

Hera. The supposed Mother of Assassins. A story told to scare children and corrupt officials alike. This man thinks she's real and that he's hired one of her people. Interesting. If I play my cards right ...

"The job was well done. I was happy to pay it to one of her people," he says in a placating tone, eyes darting.

"It was." I nod. "But *I* wouldn't have stabbed you in the shoulder if I was paid."

He scowls. "I paid. I paid enough that my purse will feel it for weeks."

Time to see if my other guess is correct.

I cock my head. "But you were healthily compensated by your ... sponsor."

Langford freezes. "What do you know about that?"

He's playing a dangerous game, getting more involved with Ellcombe—and Hera, if she's real.

"Come now, Langford, you know Hera has eyes everywhere."

He looks away. "I know."

"You still haven't told me," I push, a hint of threat entering my tone.

"What? How much I paid?"

"No," I say, taking my feet off the desk and leaning forwards. "Why she stabbed you."

"I offered her a job," he says bitterly, scowling again. "She didn't want it. What kind of assassin turns down a job?"

I don't know what I was expecting, but that certainly wasn't it. Why stab a potential employer?

"What job?" I sound too curious, but I can't take it back now.

His eyes brighten as they drift to the swords now strapped to my back. A fae man can be an imposing sight to someone of Langford's physique, even more so when he has two swords on display.

"Perhaps you would do it while you're here? Earn some extra coin."

I lean back again, ignoring the way my weapons dig in, and make myself appear thoughtful. "What's the job?"

"A babe." He smirks. "Larson Kepler's."

I force a deep breath past my teeth and into my lungs, force my chest to keep rising and falling and my face to remain interested. But internally—my blood boils. Now, now I understand how a fae could lose control of his magic. In this moment, I am glad I only have the shift.

I've been quiet for slightly too long, and Langford's brow drops in puzzlement.

"Ah." I swallow, then confirm, "And she didn't want it?"

"No!" He throws up a hand. "What kind of assassin won't kill a child? But she was ... adamant." He presses a hand to his wounded shoulder, wincing again.

"Did you see where she went?" I ask, ignoring the red in my vision. "I'll need to have a word about this indiscretion."

He sits up straighter, growing braver with my apparent approval.

"No. I thought about having her followed, but I wouldn't want to upset Hera. It's a relationship I value deeply."

"Yes," I say, standing, needing to move. "Of course. You're quite right."

Langford nods. "Can I offer you something to drink? I have some of the finest loi in the Conquered Lands."

He goes to rise.

"No, no. I'll get it." I wave him aside.

I cross to the small table by the main window, pouring a purple liquid from a pitcher into two glasses.

"Aside from the incident with the babe, you were happy with the job done?" I ask, picking up the drinks.

"Yes," he says, a hint of smugness entering his voice as he twists to speak with me. "It doesn't lead back to me at all, and my sponsors were happy."

"Good. Good."

I stop beside him, handing him a glass.

We drink together, the lord smiling.

Smacking my lips, I place my glass on the desk.

"Well, there's just one more thing." I drop my hand on Langford's shoulder. His injured shoulder. He yelps, but I tighten my grip, keeping him still. "Hera does not approve of killing infants. If I hear even a whisper of the babe's death"—I press my thumb down on the wound and the lord screams—"your own will swiftly follow."

It's not until I'm out of town, in the surrounding forest that I allow my mask to fall away, to drop the partial persona I had adopted for Lord Langford. I inhale long and deep, pulling the sweet scent of the forest deep into my lungs, erasing the dirt of the town, cleansing my soul.

A babe. She had refused to kill a child, after shredding two men to pieces and killing three others.

It seems my assassin has morals. However small.

But I still need to find her. Which means I need to get back into Southlily and pick up her trail. I can't be more than five days behind her.

I head back into town.

Southlily isn't anywhere near as large as the capital of Frigarth or Ashennor, which makes the job less daunting. Especially because there can't be more than five inns or taverns here. It's a simple matter of asking around.

I start at one end of the town and work my way down, describing my 'cousin' who had been in town within the past week. It's not until I reach a human inn that I have any success, hiding my pointed ears with a hat. A fae wouldn't stay here. It would draw too much attention, so she'd have to have stayed in disguise if at all.

"Ah, you mean Deliah!"

"Yes!" I say, slapping the inn keeper on the shoulder. "My cousin sometimes goes by her middle name."

"Lovely lass," Don says, handing me a bowl of soup. "I'm afraid you've missed her. Brother arrived—what, two days ago?"

The serving girl nods, shoving a piece of her messy hair behind her ear.

"Left right away."

Two days. Only two days.

But I can hardly ask what way they were headed. I should know that if we were meant to be travelling together. And she would hardly give her real destination to this man, any-way.

I let my shoulders slump. "I'd hoped to join them."

"A shame," he says, hurrying to serve another man.

"We have a spare room, if you need somewhere to stay the night," the girl says, her eyes large as she stares at me. I suppose covering my ears does little to detract attention from my form. I mentally shrug.

"I appreciate it, but I think I'll head on home since they're gone."

She nods, her eyes falling away from mine.

I hesitate. "Did you happen to see her brother?"

"No," she says, shrugging. "She said she'd gotten a letter."

So, am I tracking one or two people now? Is this 'brother' a made-up excuse or a fellow assassin?

I'd lean towards the first if I didn't know she'd travelled with Kyler Thames before. Or perhaps it was a messenger from this Mother of Assassins with another job.

"She offer you a room?" Don says, appearing before me again.

"Yes." I pause. "Are there any big events coming up in town? My cousin loves to attend them."

"Nah, nothing here." Don shakes his head.

"There never is," a thin man says from a beside me. "Not unless you're a lord or lady."

My stomach jumps. "Are they having a gathering soon?"

"Fundraiser," he grunts around a mouthful of stew. "In Dinas Carden. Have one ev'ry few months. Get all the important people together."

"Never see a coin from them though," Don says, gesturing around the inn at the worn wood and stained floor. It's not the cleanest inn I've seen but as a human he's lucky to have one with Ellcombe gaining more and more power.

"Goes straight to their pockets."

"Thanks ...?"

"Loyd," the man says, shaking my hand.

"Loyd. When is the next fundraiser? That Lord Langford is still here."

"A few days. No idea what Langford's doing."

"He was in last night for a drink," Don says, still listening in while the girl serves customers. "Not looking too good, is he?"

I nod along with Loyd.

So, he hasn't been nearly as discreet with his injury as he thinks. I wonder if anyone has drawn the connection to the killings yet. Maybe I'll have to help them along before I leave.

"Well," I say, pushing back my stool, "I best be off. The ole lady will be glad to see me home."

Don and Loyd mumble their goodbyes, already on to the next piece of gossip.

I mull over all I've learnt, but there's only one clear place to go. Only one option that has a direction. If I leave now, I could make it in time for the fundraiser.

Once on the edge of town, I shift, soaring into the sky. Dinas Carden it is.

9

Eilah

G ETTING INTO THE FUNCTION will be the easy part. Killing the fae lawyer without anyone suspecting foul play, and then getting out, that will be the hard part. But I do love a good challenge.

Some of the prize money from Finn buys me a dress that will do nicely, but I'll need to sew some pockets into it. I've no idea what I'll put in them yet, but pockets are a must. I book a room in an inn two blocks away, borrow a needle from the maid, and lock myself in with my new dress and some extra fabric. Heavy curtains guard me from view.

Draping the dress over my knee, I set to work. I never did understand why Mother drilled us so long on the sewing of clothes when I was young—skin yes, but fabric?—yet it's a skill I've used on nearly every job.

What I really need is a good poison. Slow acting, and not messy.

But I had to travel light on the Lord Dennel job, and the sole poison I have is much too obvious.

I pause, fixing the thread that's come loose from the eye of the needle.

I might have to get creative.

Venom? No, what snake would be found in a building packed with people? This would be so much easier if I could just kill him and all his guards. But that would draw too much attention, which is why Mother chose the fundraiser. It'll give me the chance to get close to him.

One pocket done, I reposition the dress to sew another into the other side. One can never have too many pockets.

Obviously the usual ideas are out; ice daggers, steel daggers, my usual poisons, arrows, strangulation, exsanguination.

Oh! I could wait for him to drink some water and then freeze it! As soon as I have the thought, I dismiss it. I've never been able to do that properly. It's much easier to cover the whole person in ice. Easy being a relative term here, freezing someone uses a lot of magic. Mother insists I try freezing water inside a person every time I'm back at the tower though, but I can't quite get it yet.

Perhaps he could 'slip' down the stairs? But if someone saw the ice on the stair, they'd know it was foul play. Same problem if something happened to drop on his head.

Sighing, I lower the dress to the lumpy bed beside to me. What I need is to get a good look at my target. Then I can work from there.

My target, Mivaan, is a career man, spending every moment at work. Which makes him easy to find and track even at night. The buildings of Dinas Carden sit wall to wall—or pillar to pillar since fae hate walls—and navigating the city to Mivaan's office becomes a simple stroll across the rooftops. Soldiers patrol the streets below, but not one of them glances up as I tread lightly by.

Above the open entranceway of the three-story building reads Mivaan and Co. Easy to find usually means easy to kill. But the nature of this job changes everything.

Though the building is open after the usual fae customs, curtains have been hung to offer privacy for potential clients. I can't see him. Sighing, I settle on the cold stone of the roof.

My target doesn't appear on the street until two hours after dark, and he's flanked by two guards. Whatever he's working on must be important, especially if Ellcombe want him gone.

Mivaan is a lean man, tall, with long dark hair pulled into a bun on top of his head. I cock my head. He's not what I was expecting. He's young, healthy, somewhat handsome. That might make it easier for a beautiful woman to get closer to him, but it makes a natural death less believable.

Definitely a challenge. If I have to get close to kill him, then enough time needs to have passed between our contact and when he dies that no one suspects me.

Acting on instinct, I climb down the side of the building I'm perched on and land on the cobbled stones below. Time to see what kind of man Mivaan is.

I straighten my dress, dust off the hem, and run onto the street the lawyer currently walks down, his guards a step behind him

"Help!" I yell, looking around wildly. When my eyes land on their small group, I let them widen, then run after the men, stumbling on my dress. "Help! Oh, please, help!"

Mivaan whirls around, and the two guards hold out a hand to block his way. Time to get creative.

I glance over my shoulder as though searching for an attacker and trip on my dress, sending myself sprawling across the dirty street. Mud covers my palms and sticks to my dress, and my knees offer a throb of pain.

I sob.

"Miss!" Mivaan calls, shoving his guards aside. "Are you all right?"

Oh, I am good.

I twist, frantically looking over my shoulder even as I hear Mivaan running towards me.

He reaches my side and offers me a hand, his eyes scanning the street behind me.

I grab on to him, flaring my eyes. "Oh, please. Please! There's someone following me."

He pulls me to my feet and plants himself in front of me as he continues to scan the street and buildings. Mivaan's scent washes over me, oil dotting his skin in a mix of vanilla and spices.

"What's going on?"

I jump, perhaps a little too violently, spinning to find the guards stepping up beside us, swords in hand. I whimper.

Mivaan's smooth hand squeezes mine.

"This young lady is being stalked."

"There's no one there," the first guard says, his face pinched.

I peek out from behind the lawyer.

"Perhaps we scared them off," the second guard says, his blue eyes flickering to me. "Are you all right?"

"I—" I gulp, then slowly nod. "Thank you. Thank you so much."

Apparently satisfied that his guards are on the alert, Mivaan finally turns to me, his brown eyes scanning me head to toe for injury. I follow his gaze down to my dress. It's filthy, but it was nowhere near as expensive as the one I bought for the fundraiser. And I'm willing to sacrifice it for this insight into my target.

"I suspect you may have a graze or two, but perhaps no more than that?" Mivaan says gently, his voice smooth and clear.

I nod. In fact, both of my knees were grazed in that final fall. What can I say? I'm dedicated.

"May I make sure the damage isn't severe?"

"All right," I murmur, fighting a smile at his smooth talking. Mivaan takes my arm, leading me to the nearest building and helps me sit on a step.

"Your pardon," he says, carefully pulling my dress up to above my knees. "Ah," Mivaan says, "the blood has already stopped and the wounds are clean."

"I'm just thankful you were here to scare him away. I don't know what I would have done." I bury my face in my hands.

"Come, there's no need for that. You're safe now." He pauses. "But perhaps we can walk you home?"

"Oh." I drop my hands, letting my eyes light marginally. "Would you? I don't want to be alone."

He smiles, helping me to my feet and offering me his arm. I take it with a small smile.

"I'm staying at the Enchanted Tree." I'm not. But it's a reputable inn, one someone attending the fundraiser might be staying in.

Mivaan sets off, his guards falling in behind us silently.

"I'm Mivaan," he says, his voice still soft as though I might scare.

"Deliah," I say, the false name rolling of my tongue. It's one of my favourites.

"What were you doing out late by yourself, Deliah? Dinas Carden isn't safe at night."

I wince. "I'm in the city to visit family, and we were going to go down to the markets, but we got separated on the way, and then that—that man started following me!"

"Your family must be worried," Mivaan says.

I look down, the picture of perfect chastisement settling on my face. "I'll have a message sent to them as soon as I'm back at the inn."

I pause, sending a tentative glance his way. A rescued damsel showing interest in her saviour is not unusual, and I need to pique his interest in me. "What about you? Why are you out so late, sir?"

He smiles. "I'm working on a case."

"A case?" I inspect the guards behind us and frown. "Are you an officer?"

Mivaan laughs. "No, I'm a lawyer."

"Oh."

"Oh?"

I look up at him sheepishly. "You don't look like a lawyer."

He doesn't. Not with the almost casual tunic he wears, the dark pants, and high bun. Interesting.

He laughs, this time loudly. "I don't? Well perhaps, I don't enjoy the normal look."

I give him a shy smile as though encouraged by his words. "No, this is much better."

We round a corner and the Enchanted Tree appears before Mivaan can say anything more but the smile still on his face says more than enough.

"Thank you," I say, reluctantly sliding my arm free. I make sure my hand lingers on his arm for a moment.

Mivaan's eyes are glued to mine, uncaring of all else. Perfect.

"Would you forgive me if I said it was a pleasure to find you in such distress? I enjoyed walking you home."

I smile. "Yes, because I'd have to agree."

The guards shift and Mivaan gives my hand a squeeze. "We'll leave you here, Deliah. Make sure you have someone clean those knees."

And they disappear down the dark street, Mivaan glancing over his shoulder with a smile.

And I know just how I'm going to kill him.

10

Raiden

I ARRIVE IN DINAS Carden the day of the fundraiser. Securing an invitation is as simple as flashing the royal seal of Frigarth, an item Laurel and Turin see that I'm never without while searching for their daughter.

I set up in the Enchanted Tree, a reputable inn a block from where the function is to take place. It was clear as soon as I walked in that I'm not their sole patron attending the fundraiser tonight.

The function is due to start at dusk. If the assassin is planning something, I need to be there early. But I can't take my swords. I can't take anything. The invitation is clear on the security there. So I'll have to find another way to stop her.

Dressed in all black, I head over with half an hour to spare. The function is being held in a large manor, belonging to Lord Braeden of Dinas Carden. But when I arrive, admissions inside have already opened.

I join the line, scanning the front of the grey building as I pretend to straighten my new tunic. It's four stories high, completely open, with a balcony on each level and not a guard in sight above the ground floor. I wouldn't be surprised if the assassin is already inside.

"Invitation?"

I pull the piece of paper from my tunic and hand it over. The man's eyes light with interest. It's not often Frigarth comes to the Conquered Lands officially, not with Ellcombe's increasing presence. But we're not officially at war, though tensions continue to rise.

"Go ahead," the guard finally says, waving me through.

Nodding my thanks, I climb the stairs and enter the main hall.

The manor is a cruel display of wealth in a nation on its knees, and it's clear there isn't merely one person responsible for putting it there. Ellcombe may have taken this land, but its lords continue to hand it to them as they fill their own pockets while humans serve them against their will.

I wonder who the assassin is after, there's no shortage of potential targets and I'm sure she's here.

The ceiling depicts a painting of a forest scene, with starlight gems embedded in the leaves of the trees and in the eyes of the deer running across the mural.

I follow the crowd into the ballroom, exchanging greetings with various officials and their families. None of them appear particularly concerned about my presence, though interest lights in their eyes. Word of where I'm from has passed around. This fundraiser could be good for more than finding the assassin. I might learn something about Ellcombe's movements, too. I make careful note of the people who try their best to move away from me subtly.

A rounded fae man takes the large, marble staircase that leads to the next level and clears his throat, tapping a spoon against his glass.

"Honoured guests," he calls, but the crowd continues to gossip. "Honoured guests!"

Slowly the voices quieten. A soft breeze floats through the open room, fanning dresses and coats alike, spreading the scent of the cakes and desserts lining the border of the extravagant room.

"Thank you for joining me in my humble home." At this there is a quiet chuckle from the crowd. It's with effort that I offer a smile.

"Ladies, gentleman, you know the drill. Eat and drink to your heart's content, and don't forget to empty your pockets before you leave!"

Lord Braeden gives one loud clap, and the dozen musicians across the room launch into a lively tune as he rejoins the growing crowd.

I trace the border of the ballroom, marked by the curtains draped around it and the tables of food, scanning every woman's face. I never saw the assassin's, but I'd recognise those eyes anywhere. If she's still in the country, this is where she'll be. I spot at least five of her potential targets within minutes but not her.

As the musicians swap to another song, their strings echoing through the room, pairs take the dance floor. Still, I keep searching. I can rule out the women wading through the crowd, trays clutched in their hands. Their curved ears are carefully, obviously displayed, bands of iron on their ankles. My blood heats at the sight, and I have to wrench my eyes away.

My eyes land on a young woman in a dark blue dress, her long brown hair braided down her back. The length of it gives me pause. *Her* hair was nearly that long. Down to the small of her back. I study the girl. Her arms are muscled, her form clearly lean despite the layers of fabric. She's very tanned, more than most of the other ladies here.

Walking to the right, I try to get a glimpse of her face. Her eyes. Those are what will give her away.

She smiles as she speaks to another lady, nodding politely as they exchange a few words. Her lips are layered in dark red.

I take one more step and my heart jumps.

Eyes like a stormy sea.

It's her. The assassin.

11

Eilah

H E'S BEEN STARING AT me for nineteen minutes and thirty-three seconds. Not Mivaan. Not one of the other lords or councillors or important people that I'm sure Ellcombe wouldn't miss. No. It's the soldier from Frigarth, his eyes cloudy with suppressed anger. Guess that little warning I left him two years ago didn't last. Should have known. Mercy always comes back to bite you.

I excuse myself from Lady Braeden, offering a small curtsy as I turn away. I don't look at the soldier, dressed in a sleek black suit that shows his muscled form. No need to let him know I recognised him, not when I need to work out why he's here. I weave my way through the crowd, offering demure smiles as I pass a group of men by the drinks table. Still no sign of Mivaan.

The soldier's blue eyes follow me.

The real question, I think as I take a delicate glass full of a silver liquid, is whether this man is here for me or the fundraiser. Kyler wasn't exactly the most difficult target to follow, not with the way he left his victims, and I'm sure that was the only reason he caught up with us. But it can't be coincidence that this soldier is here now when Kyler is dead. Kyler did have his uses, though. I shove the thought away before my mind can lead me down the path to Sorren and what Kyler did to him for me.

I need to focus on the task at hand.

Perhaps I can find a way to use the soldier to my advantage tonight. I grin. Oh yes, having him unwittingly help me could be fun.

"Excuse me, miss, I hope you don't mind me saying, but you look exquisite tonight."

I turn, feigning embarrassment as I find myself face-to-face with an older fae man. Usually fae prefer those closer to their own physical appearance of age. But this man has grey hair and eye wrinkles.

"Oh, thank you, sir." I shift, unsure if I want to hear his request, but I also need to blend in.

"Perhaps I might ask for a dance? Unless you are other-wise entertained." He leans closer. "I would greatly appreci-ate a rescue, miss. Lord Quincy has been pestering me about a new tax on dye for the past week, and I am keen to evade him tonight."

I laugh. Taxes!

"I would be glad to rescue you, sir," I say, honestly. A dance with no strings attached is exactly what I need.

He sighs, relief spreading across his old face, and my smile turns genuine.

I take his weathered hand as I see the eager eyes of another fae man land on him—Lord Quincy, no doubt—and lead him to the makeshift dance floor in the centre of the room. His eyes shine with mirth as we take our places.

"Forgive me, miss, I believe I didn't introduce myself. I am Hadley."

Not a lord ... perhaps another lawyer? I take his arm as his hand slips to my waist.

"Deliah," I say as we move through the lively steps of the dance. Mother makes sure we all know the most popular dances.

I can still feel the eyes of the soldier on me, and Hadley's follower hangs on the sidelines. But I ignore them both. It's a rare day that I can have an interaction without an ulterior motive, and with Mivaan still not here, I can do exactly that.

"Are you from Dinas Carden, Deliah?" Hadley asks, pausing as he swirls me out. My long braid whirls out around me, my skirt flourishing with the movement. I quite enjoy the sensation.

"I'm visiting family," I say as I stop before him again. "My aunt is late, though."

He nods sympathetically but doesn't ask any more about my story. If Mivaan is late, I'm sure many others are.

"So," I say after a pause, "taxes."

"Oh, please no," Hadley laughs.

A genuine giggle escapes me. "But it sounds like such riveting conversation."

"Lord Quincy certainly thinks so, but I find it all rather dull."

I nod, but I can hardly tell him what I do for entertainment. Instead, I cast a glance upwards, at a mural that outshines the one in the main hall. "I always wondered how such beautiful paintings could be completed on a ceiling."

"A true feat." Hadley's eyes twinkle. "You have an interest in art?"

"Oh, yes." I smile. "Art can tell you a lot about a person."

The song comes to an end and I casually peek over Hadley's shoulder. "It appears safe now, sir. Lord Quincy has accosted some other poor fellow."

Hadley laughs, following my gaze. "I am in your debt, Deliah."

"Come find me again if you need another rescue." Perhaps a mistake, but I would happily help him again.

We part ways, and I'm forced to face reality as Mivaan arrives.

The game continues. And it's a long one.

"You can't seem to get your eyes off me, soldier," I say, offering him a small smile. In flat shoes, I'm barely shorter than him, but his form is strong and broad. "Perhaps you'd like to dance?"

His head cocks, his eyes flicking between me and over my shoulder at Hadley as he walks away. Intrigued. He's intrigued. I silently thank the old fae for confusing the soldier with our interaction.

"Raiden," he says. "Raiden Elvar."

"A pleasure." I purr.

He lets me take his hand, his skin warm and rough, and lead him to the dance floor as I did Hadley.

"You dance well," Elvar says as we wait for the next song, couples surrounding us.

"Are you admitting to watching me, soldier?" I let my own eyes wash over him, taking in his strong form, short pale blond hair and those piercing eyes again. I let my own linger on his abdomen where I left my mark. "We've danced before."

But he doesn't shift under my gaze. He merely nods.

I step closer to him as the slower song begins, wrapping my arms around his neck, placing my mouth by his ear as we sway. He doesn't appear rattled by my closeness, so I let my hand drift up to his hair. It's slightly longer than the last time I saw him, almost outside of regulation.

"Are you armed?"

Elvar doesn't respond, and I laugh.

"I'm sorry. I shouldn't play with you like that."

"Why are you here?" His tone is firm, but not rude.

I let my hand fall from his soft hair, offering him a coy look.

"Can't I enjoy a party?" We say nothing for a moment as he leads me through the more complicated moves of the dance, the music wafting around us like a warm embrace. "Why are *you* here?"

As if I didn't know. He's not exactly subtle with that stare.

"I'm sure you've guessed."

I smile, nodding as though nothing is wrong, as though I am not concerned. Which isn't hard because this man can do nothing to me, but it is a show for those around us. I lean in close to Elvar again, as though enjoying the dance, but I've spotted Mivaan over his shoulder. The young lawyer skirts the dance floor, walking with no clear destination, eyes forwards but mind clearly elsewhere.

I subtly change our path, bury my hand inside my pocket as though holding my skirt up.

"You did well finding me. I'll give you that. But then, you have an advantage," I say, and this time I feel his body stiffen for a moment before relaxing. Yes, he's still a little sore on the subject after all. But a wound like that, a unique wound … that's what he used to find me. He's a smart one. Should have killed him when I had the chance.

"Let's make this quick, soldier," I mutter. "I don't fancy getting this dress bloody, so it seems you've been given one more chance to escape with your life; leave me alone."

"And escape the pleasure of your company?" He smiles, not quite reaching his eyes. "After you answer my question."

I frown. "I did."

"Not that one." He shakes his head, still effortlessly leading me through the steps. Impressive for a soldier. "Kyler Thames. Was he in Frigarth seventeen years ago?"

Anger flares in my stomach at the mention of the country, but I force my expression to remain unchanged. Of course this is about Frigarth. But I have nothing to say. They deserved whatever Kyler did.

"You already know the answer to that question. If you're searching for more confirmation, you're wasting your time."

Besides, I don't know anything about Kyler's missions. And Mother keeps the details of that particular one secret, more so after our run in with Elvar and his soldiers. Too many of our people were there, and the risk for us is great if their names got out. Besides, our dealings with Frigarth aren't over.

"Did he take her?"

I frown, cocking my head and studying his face. So, he's looking for someone. But I don't care, and a glance over his shoulder shows Mivaan is getting close. I need to end this conversation now. I don't know the details, but I can certainly make sure this man leaves me alone.

"Whoever you're looking for is dead, soldier. We're assassins," I hiss, watching my words hit their mark.

Satisfaction drips down my spine at the pain that flares in his eyes as his grip goes stiff. He stares unseeingly at the scar on my chin, unable to hold my gaze.

"Now, be a gentleman and leave me alone."

Mivaan draws level with us, closer than even I could have planned, and completely oblivious to my dancing merely steps away from him. I pull back from Raiden, and purposely fumble my steps. I trip on my skirt and gasp.

It happens in the blink of an eye, but that's all I need. I go careening into Mivaan, our bodies slamming together with such force that we go sprawling to the ground. I land on top of him, and before he's had a moment to collect himself, I've pumped a syringe full of air into his veins.

"Ow." Mivaan grunts, but then his brown eyes clear and brighten as they land on mine. "Deliah?"

"Mivaan?" I groan, dropping my eyes. "I'm so sorry."

"Not at all," he says with a grin, his arms gripping me. "But perhaps we might get up from the floor?"

"Oh, right," I say, glancing around sheepishly.

My shadow's eyes have narrowed on me, but Mivaan is still alive and, to all appearances, unhurt.

I stumble to my feet and Mivaan steadies me as I straighten my skirt.

"I think your brooch got me," Mivaan says, rubbing at his hand.

I frown, inspecting my dress. The small silver pin is unclipped, the sharp end sticking out as planned. I resist the smile that threatens to raise my lips and force my eyes to widen.

"I'm so sorry," I say, grabbing his hand. A small pinprick of blood has beaded on his skin, but it's not my broach that did it. I send a silent thanks towards Mother for always insisting on the importance of pockets.

Mivaan is now a ticking time bomb. But it won't be poison or venom that kills him. He's going to die from heart failure—perhaps a stroke—when the air bubbles reach his heart. And my little pinprick will exonerate me when there is no trace of poison found.

"It's nothing," he says, smiling. "I was just thinking of you. Has there been any sign of the man following you last night?"

I hesitate, wondering if it's worth mentioning my soldier, but I shake my head. I don't want him to get involved. Who knows what he might say, and I really don't need the hassle.

"No. I have to thank you again. You must have scared him away."

"Then maybe we can finish this dance together?" His eyes are shining, locked on me. Enraptured.

"I would like that." In fact, nearly all the other dancing pairs have stopped to stare, and Elvar stands to the side, his eyes darting between me and Mivaan. We need to end this scene I created.

I pull my brooch free, stuffing it into my pocket in a move that lets me cap the syringe and prevent it from stabbing me in the leg.

"Please excuse me," I say over my shoulder to Elvar as the music begins again. And Mivaan and I join the dancers.

We dance most of the night, except for when I excuse myself under the watchful eye of Elvar, aiming for another man. But then I appear to change my mind, glancing sideways at my handsome shadow in the corner. I spin around, heading back to Mivaan. Let the soldier think I'm too afraid to kill under his gaze. Let him think I don't have a chance when I've already succeeded.

It's almost a shame that Mivaan is going to die. He's nothing but a gentleman the entire night. But so was Sorren. My heart gives a sharp throb. No, Mivaan doesn't deserve my pity. I stamp my emotions down. He's nothing more than a step towards a larger goal.

We part ways in the early morning, along with the other lords, ladies, and important people of the Conquered Lands stumbling down the front steps of the manor. My shadow vanishes among them, and this time, I don't feel his eyes on me.

12

Raiden

I DON'T SLEEP AT all, perched on the high roof of an inn, my room at the Enchanted Tree forgotten.

Dead.

Her words echo in my mind, bouncing back and forth until the darkness recedes and an orange dawn slowly arrives on the horizon.

She said Zara was dead.

And yet, my brain whispers. *And yet.*

Her answer doesn't sit.

Why take the princess if the aim was assassination? And then, once the job was done, why not advertise it?

We're assassins.

And yet.

I ruffle my feathers, shaking away my whirling thoughts, scanning the lightening street below. There's no sign of her yet, but already the sleeping city is waking up. And with it, news.

People gather in clumps outside buildings, in the middle of the streets, and along cobbled pathways. Boys run from house to house, shouting the latest gossip to the occupants.

Mivaan, a fae lawyer, is dead. A heart attack, they say. The man *she* danced with all night.

I'm sure she did it. I don't know how—the doctor declared his blood free of poison.

But he's dead.

And she danced with him all night.

And yet.

I scan the street again, waiting for her form to appear. Deliah, he called her. No doubt a fake name, but I find it stuck in my mind. A persistent reminder of her.

Kyler Thames is dead.

Zara is dead.

And I must tell my king and queen.

And yet.

But I promised I would return with their daughter, dead or alive, and I intend to keep it. Deliah has one more question to answer before I can return home.

If Zara is dead, then where is her body?

I've never been so close.

Deliah's lean form appears below, dressed in loose fitting black pants and a pale yellow shirt. A bag strapped to her back. She struts from the small inn I'd followed her to, pausing and cocking her head for a moment, before continuing on her way. She doesn't stop or stumble as a boy yells the news to her. Doesn't appear shocked or surprised. I doubt she even blinks.

I let her reach the end of the narrow street before flying after her, keeping above the open buildings where the air is fresh and there's less chance of being noticed.

The assassin moves confidently, with the ease of a fighter. She is someone intricately aware of her physical capabilities. I'll need to be careful if she can kill so easily without suspicion or remorse. I keep on her tail.

Deliah makes only one stop to collect a grey horse from the stables on the edge of town. She doesn't hesitate as she steps through the wide western gate of Dinas Carden, the horse trailing behind her with her bag strapped to the saddle. She doesn't squirm under the eyes of the guards. Doesn't look back. And she doesn't look up.

Two hours out of Dinas Carden, my wings still going strong, Deliah stops with a dramatic sigh that my rook's eyes can see even at a distance. She twists in the saddle, her eyes locking on me, and pats the rump of the mare in invitation.

I caw a laugh. I should have known she wouldn't be so easy to follow. After a moment's debate, I decide to humour her. I land on the horse. It doesn't flinch.

"An apt form," the assassin mutters, twisted in her seat to stare down at me. Daggers rest on her hips, but I doubt she uses them much. She has no need with her magic.

I hop to the ground with a flutter, shifting in moments to stand before her, arms crossed. The forest stretches away behind us, open grass in front.

"Back again, soldier?" Deliah says, a slight frown crinkling her brow. She tucks a long strand of hair behind her ear. "This is getting tiresome."

I give her a smirk, matching her demeanour. "Couldn't stay away."

"Hmph." She squeezes her knees and abruptly sends the horse into a trot. But before I can take a step after her, she flings her arm out behind her. A spear of ice shoots towards me faster than I can blink. It scrapes along my cheek, the icy cold drawing warm blood. I fight a shiver at the memory it provokes.

Deliah grins over her shoulder, her long hair whipping around her. "Next time I won't miss."

She means it as a threat. But I decide to see it as a challenge. Shifting, I race after her, my wings cutting through the air, pushing me on and on until I'm ahead of her. I land, twisting the magic inside so that I'm a man again when she reaches me.

The assassin draws the horse to a halt again, glaring.

"I need to know who else was there."

She huffs, her breath fog on the air though it's a warm day.

"I can't help you," Deliah snaps, her sea-green eyes flashing.

"Why not?" An edge has crept into my voice, but I don't fight it. I need to know. I need to find Zara. I *have* to.

A slight frown crinkles her brow as she stares into my eyes, as if she's wondering what to say or whether it would just be easier to kill me. I remind myself to be careful, but I'm so close to knowing. Closer than I've ever been.

"I don't know who was there," she finally mutters, her fingers twitching on the reins. The mare doesn't move.

"Please," I say, stepping up to the horse's side.

"I told you"—she pushes the mare away from me with her knee—"assassins don't kidnap."

"She was a child!" I say, desperation clear in my voice now. "An infant. She has to be alive."

Her perfect mask flickers for a moment, and I remember what Lord Langford said. She doesn't kill children.

"Who?"

"I—" She really doesn't know what I'm talking about? "The princess."

"I don't know anything about the mission," she growls, her mask back in place, temper flaring.

"Then point me to someone who does."

Deliah's eyes snap upwards as a hawk flies overhead, its soft trill echoing down to us. A distant expression crosses her face, as though this conversation bores her.

"Deliah!" I snap, grabbing the mare's reins.

Her eyes whip to mine and though she wields ice, her eyes are on fire. "Be grateful I've let you live this long, shadow. I have places to be, people to kill. Be a good little soldier and go home." She grins wickedly. "Maybe I'll even see you there one day soon."

13

Eilah

MY LITTLE SOLDIER IS persistent, I'll give him that.

He may have dropped back to barely within eye-sight, but he's still there. Still following from the sky as the hard ground whips by underneath me. Raiden Elvar.

I should have killed him years ago.

I should have killed him last night.

And I should have killed him today.

But there's something in those eyes. Something in the way he's tracked me down that stops me.

It's the desperation.

The sickening, disgusting, gut wrenching desperation.

But if he gets in my way, no amount of sad puppy eyes will stop me from putting him down.

I have a job to do.

And besides, he's from Frigarth. If I'm going to tear that kingdom to the ground, I can't have him trailing along after me looking for some long dead child. Even if he is easy on the eyes.

A child. I sigh, pushing the mare faster. Mother's never shied away from tough jobs when circumstances demanded and, I'll admit, killing the princess would have been a good blow to the kingdom. But ... a child.

I shake my head, lean further into the saddle, and push the mare on. I lose myself in the speed and the pure exhilaration of riding so fast I seem to fly. There's a reason I travel by horse rather than my own shifted form. The snow leopard can't run this fast for this long. Its only use is for killing. Huh, guess I have an apt form, too.

I keep the fast pace for as long as I can across the next two days, pushing the mare as far as possible without hurting her. My mind goes in circles, bouncing between Elvar, Aeris, and the child Mother had killed, unable to shake the thoughts that haunt me.

When I finally pull the mare back to a walk to cross the first of many winding rivers on the southern outskirts of Frigarth, I don't bother searching the skyline for my shadow again. He'll be far behind now. I can't help but hope I won't see him and his sad eyes again. Perhaps the draw of being so close to home will pull him away from me now.

"All right, Horse," I say, slipping from the saddle on the muddy bank of the slow river. "Drink up."

No use giving her a proper name. I can hardly take her back home with me. A horse doesn't belong in the desert. I absentmindedly stroke her neck as she drinks her fill, snorting deep breaths between gulps.

A child.

Urgh! Why am I letting this man's worries have a place in my mind? That was seventeen years ago. I can hardly change anything now. Besides, I should be happy.

It made Frigarth hurt. And that's what I want. That's what I've been raised for. They're the reason I was pushed so much harder than the others, the reason I've been killing for so much longer. The reason I've suffered so much more.

Yes. It's a good thing the girl was killed.

Unclipping my waterskin from the saddle, I bend to fill it up in the clear, cold water. And finally notice what I should have six minutes ago.

The soft crunch of a boot on twigs.

The smell of a sweaty body on the wind. Coming from the opposite direction to the boot.

Raiden Elvar may be gone. But I've picked up some other followers, hiding in the short scrub and low bushes around me.

If I ever see that man again, I'm blaming him for the distraction that's cost me precious minutes.

Stupid soldier.

It takes me a second to make the realisation of the men closing in from at least two sides. I haven't flinched, haven't paused, I merely keep filling my waterskin, listening intently. Without moving my head, I scan what little I can see to either side of me. Movement catches in my right peripheral.

Oh, there are a lot more than two men here.

This, this is going to be fun.

But to let them know I know they're there, or spring their deaths on them as the surprise it's sure to be?

The mare finally senses the men surrounding us, her head rising with a jolt and a nervous whinny, and taking the fun of the decision from my hands.

"What is it, girl?" I murmur, rising with her, pulling on my magic, letting it rise to my fingertips. Ready.

My eyes lock on those of a burly, red-haired fae as he steps out from behind a tree directly in front of me.

My grin is the last thing he sees. That and the ice dagger flying for his face.

I don't watch his body fall to the ground, whirling around, aiming and releasing another dagger in seconds.

My target sends a gust of wind into it, strong enough to knock it off course, but the ice still buries deep into his shoulder.

His screams chase the mare as she runs. But she has my bag. Sighing, I send a dagger after her, even as I spin to take in the odds.

Fae men step out from behind scrub, bushes, and trees around me. Oh, if Mother ever hears of how many men I've let sneak up on me now, she will be furious. The punishment would be the worst I've ever had ...

Ten. There are ten.

But I give them a wicked grin. Sometimes even I can't tell the difference between false and real confidence.

"Oh, someone knows who I am."

A dark-haired, dark-skinned fae steps forwards. "And Cicia of Ellcombe wants you to know it."

Ah. Cicia. I wonder if she knows I killed her snivelling son last year on her queen's orders.

"One question," I say, holding up a finger, an ice dagger gripped in my hand. "How'd you find me? You understand, I can't have that happening again."

Again, again.

Stupid soldier.

"My lady was a guest at the fundraiser you attended. She saw you entering and left immediately."

The hawk. The hawk I saw wasn't a hawk, and it wasn't my sister with a new message.

It was one of these men keeping track of which way I was headed. Which means one of them is also a telepath.

I shrug, problem solved.

"Shall we get to it, then?"

I don't wait for him to respond, but fling my dagger at his left eye. I follow close behind, and sure enough, the one with wind magic manages to push it aside. But it doesn't matter. I'm on their leader a second later. He dodges masterfully, wielding a short sword with perfect ease. I duck his slash at my neck, land in a crouch, and spin to kick his feet out from under him.

The air leaves his lungs in a rush, but I can't follow through before another man comes from behind. I roll away, mud soaking through my shirt, and send a rush of sharp ice at a different opponent as I rise to my feet. His battered and bloodied body falls backwards into a bush.

I need to be careful how much magic I use. No more ice darts unless the opportunity is too good to pass up. Magic is a long game.

I spin as the second man follows me, slashing at his abdomen. His forward momentum carries him straight into my blade, gutting him.

The men are trying to take me one at a time. They know I could tear them all to shreds in one go if they stand too close together. Lord Dennel certainly sent a message far and wide.

But fighting one man at a time is hardly a challenge.

Another man jumps forwards from my right, while one comes from my left. OK, scratch that, they're not entirely witless.

Wind whips at my body, but the injured man watching from the sidelines hardly has enough magic to cause any damage. Push a dagger, yes, but knock me off my feet? No.

He's more annoying than anything else.

But I leave him be as I take in the two men circling me. Brown Eyes and Fat Lips. Ha, I make myself laugh.

Brown Eyes sends a testing jab my way with his spear, while Fat Lips shifts his grip on his sword.

I spread my arms wide. "Come on, boys. I've got places to be."

The dark-skinned man walks into my view behind Fat Lips, eyes darkening as they land on me.

"Do it!" he growls, jolting them into action.

They pounce.

I focus on dodging, learning their styles, their weaknesses as they try and fail to land blow after blow.

It's not until a scratch opens up on my forearm that I kill Fat Lips. But Leader Man takes his place.

My magic could kill them. But it takes concentration to perform any stunt that would kill multiple enemies on more than one side. Concentration that they're not letting me get. I could try it, but it would be a risk, and I have rules about those.

Growling, I kick out Brown Eye's knee, hearing a satisfying snap, and bury my blade in his neck.

I tear it free as he slumps to the ground and throw it at Leader Man in one clean motion. Wind Boy pushes it aside.

I fix my stare on him, watching as the blood drips from his shoulder. Sweat has beaded on his brow. He hasn't got much left in him. His magic will begin to falter soon. I doubt these men are used to wielding their magic under physical duress the way Mother trained me.

I cock my head. "You look tired."

His eyes snap to something behind me, and I spin, lifting my weapon at the last moment, as Leader Man runs into it. But his own weapon was raised, and begins to fall even as his body tips backwards. I release the dagger in his heart, and step back, but it's too late. His sword slams into my shoulder, the tip dragging along my collar bone.

He crumples at my feet. Blood soaks my shirt.

It's my right shoulder. My good arm. But Mother made sure I could fight equally as well with my left, and I palm another ice dagger, gritting my teeth against the pain. Kneel or fight.

Fight now, pain later.

Wind Boy gives me a grin that almost matches the one I gave him before.

Oh, I am going to cut that smile right from his face.

Screw using my left arm. I'm ready to use my teeth.

The remaining men have been staring with satisfied smiles at the blood leaking from my shoulder, no doubt using it to psyche themselves up. Too bad it gives me enough time to let the beast out.

White and black striped fur sprouts across my skin as my body folds over and elongates. Canines sprout from my mouth, a tail from the base of my spine. And I rise before them a snow leopard.

Wind Boy's face actually pales.

I spring easily at him despite my injured shoulder, my front legs slamming into his chest. I'm sure his back breaks as he hits the ground. It's with a casual swipe of my claws that I end his life.

These men are dedicated, I'll give them that, because not one of them has fled. I can smell their fear, a sharp tang on the fresh air. Maybe now ...

I snarl my challenge, eyes flickering between the remaining five men as I bare my teeth.

Two things happen then.

All five charge.

And a rook lands beside me, sprouting into my handsome shadow the moment before the fae enclose us.

OK, so perhaps I let him take the lead out of mere curiosity. But he moves like a piece of art. Each movement the delicate strokes of a painter, each strike the lines in a pencilled sketch. I'd forgotten how talented he was when we fought. Art. He is art.

A blade whizzing barely an inch past my eye snaps me from my thoughts and I send my claws straight through the man's wrist. I ignore the feeling of bone and tendon and leap onto a nearby form, using his body as a spring pad into another one. The clash of steel on steel sounds behind me, and a glance back shows Elvar fighting the remaining two with both his swords. A dance. A dance and a piece of artwork at once. The sun glints off his blades, his eyes shining just as bright as he whirls and strikes, ducks and stabs.

Not bad.

I turn my attention back to the man I'd jumped from when a high-pitched ringing sounds in my ears. No, in my mind.

The telepath.

Oh, Mother really will be furious.

The sound is debilitating, halting me in my steps. I'm helpless as the man unsteadily rises to his feet, blood leaking from the holes my claws left in him.

I growl, baring my teeth in a move that's more grimace than threat. And he knows it.

His dark eyes narrow, and the pain grows, the sound a screech that tears through my mind, threatens to undo me.

Kneel or fight.

Roaring now, I crouch.

I'll have one chance. One hope of ending this man. There's no time to shift, no time to will the magic to work for me, and then do it again with my ice.

No, my teeth and claws will do just fine.

I let the tension build, the power ready and waiting in my legs to launch me forwards.

The telepath's smile widens, thinking I am cowering, thinking I am done. His eyes flicker towards Elvar, but I can still hear fighting. He will be of no use now. It's just me, as it always has been.

"Cicia promised a fortune," he murmurs, stepping forwards. "And now, with so many of the others gone, my share will make me a very wealthy man."

Money will do that, imbecile, I shout in my mind, wondering if he'll hear it while he's in there.

The frown that crosses his face gives me more than a little satisfaction.

Another step.

His blond hair falls over his face, sticking to his sweaty skin, but he doesn't notice so transfixed on me.

I force myself to take deep breaths through the pain, the noise a knife stabbing over and over again. One more step, that's all I need him to take. One more, and he's mine.

But he's quite happy in his gloating. His smile widening as he watches me labouring to breathe.

Screw it, I think, and force the most pitiful sound I can conjure through my sharp teeth. The stab to my pride is nearly as bad as the pain in my head, but a girl's gotta do what a girl's gotta do.

He laughs. Actually laughs and I know I am going to tear him apart when he finally takes that step.

The glint of a knife flashes in his hand.

And his bare foot rises.

And he steps closer.

Surprise! I scream at the knives in my brain, and pounce.

14

Raiden

I FINALLY HAVE THE upper hand on the two fae men, when a sound rises above the clang of swords that threatens to stop me in my tracks.

A whimper.

And coming from her, it sparks a fear deep inside.

But I can't spare the snow leopard more than a glance, which reveals her to be crouching on the ground in pain, before I'm forced to dodge a blade slashing for my face. I need to end this now. I need to help her. Or I'll lose Zara forever.

I spin, sending my swords out in a whirlwind as I drop, gaining precious space and time. The fae fall back and I roll.

If I had Deliah's magic I could send it into these men right now, but I've long come to terms with my limitations. I sprint for a tree, one of the men on my heels. Leaping into the air, I push off the trunk, spinning in place to bring my blades down upon the unsuspecting man. He's dead before he hits the ground.

I risk another glance at Deliah right as she leaps at the man standing over her, claws bared and jaw agape. And then I'm running at the other man, sliding to the ground and kicking his feet out from under him.

Scrambling forwards, I'm on him before he can draw air into his lungs, sliding a sword across his throat.

Silence descends, broken only by my ragged breathing and that of a large beast. I don't let myself dwell on the mercenaries.

"Deliah!"

Sheathing my blades, I race to her, my bare feet sinking in the thick mud. The big cat wobbles away from what's left of the man, blood coating her white fur.

Her shifted form is bigger than Jorai's large cat, and the sight of it makes my stomach jump. But the beast isn't a real animal. I drop to a crouch beside her, scanning her form as she fixes me with those fierce green eyes. I can't tell what blood is hers and what isn't.

"Shift back," I say. "I can't help you in this form."

Her lip curls revealing bloodied teeth, a soft growl escaping, but she closes her eyes.

And I wait.

"De—"

Her form finally begins to shrink, her fur swiftly disappearing as though being consumed by her skin, and her own limbs reform.

Deliah sits before me, gasping, sweat sheening on her brow, and blood on her mouth and neck. Clumps of her brown hair have pulled free from her braid, sticking to her face.

"I don't need your help," she snaps, eyes flying open as she fixes me with a fierce expression.

"Funny, because you looked like you needed it before," I say, irked.

She glares, wiping her arm across her bloodied mouth. It only smudges the mess more. She spits out a glob.

"Well, this has been fun," Deliah says dismissively. "Safe travels, soldier."

But the assassin's face pales dangerously as she pushes her feet under her.

"You're not going anywhere alone in this condition," I say simply, studying the wound now visible on her shoulder, an idea forming.

"And you're going to help me?" Deliah practically spits, swaying on her feet. The wound is deeper than she expected, that much is clear, and whatever the last man did to her has left her weak.

I make a show of looking around at the bodies. "Do you see anyone else?"

Who knew helping an assassin would be so difficult?

She barks a laugh and her resolve falters, her face flickering.

"Fine," she says bitterly, shoving hair back from her face. "But not here. There might be more coming."

"More?"

"What can I say? I enjoy having powerful enemies," she preens.

We need to leave quickly. *Her horse!* I look around for the animal, wondering what happened to it, and find its corpse on the other side of the river. Ice, now melted, has pierced her body. I sigh, raising an eyebrow at Deliah.

The assassin shrugs, her face now a perfect mask as she glances between me and her horse. "She had my bag."

"Guess we're walking," I sigh.

Wading across the stream, the slowly running water coming up to my thighs, I untie her leather bag from the mare and sling it over my shoulder. It's surprisingly light, I'd have thought an assassin would carry more with her. I spare the horse a glance, what a waste, but Deliah at least made it quick.

I make my way back to Deliah, who hasn't moved.

The assassin stares at me, a slight crinkle in her brow. She's debating asking for help. But her bloodied lips stay firmly closed. We'll be here for hours at this rate. And I'm not adding hours onto the years of waiting I've already done.

Sighing again, I sweep her off her feet.

"You could have just offered me a shoulder," she grumbles, pain making the words tight.

"A thank you would suffice."

"My knight in shining armour."

At that, I roll my eyes.

I carry her for three hours, searching for a place where we can hole up so I can treat her wounds and get the blood and gore from her skin. My arms ache from the two days of following her in rook form, the fight, and now carrying her. But I don't stop. And I don't let myself think about who she is, what she is, or what she's done. To me, to Mivaan, and to countless others. Right now, she is the person I need to find Zara, so I push it all from my mind, and pretend someone else is in my arms.

Deliah's eyes have begun to glaze, a steady sheen coating her skin, by the time I push through a dense clump of bushes and trees to find a small, grassy clearing. We'll need a fire and the forest will hide it from view, the leaves filtering the smoke.

She grunts as I lower her to the ground, wayward strands of hair clinging to her face, and slams her fist into my arm.

"What was that for?" I sit back on my heels.

"Following me," she gasps, pulling her shirt and a wad of cloth away from her shoulder, but she can't crane her neck to see the wound.

"You wouldn't be alive if I hadn't." And I would have lost my only lead on the princess. The thought sends a thread of panic through my body.

Deliah raises her chin, fire and ice somehow both in her eyes. "I would."

"Sure." I bat her hand away from her shoulder. "Lie down."

She throws me a glare, but does as I say. Like pulling teeth. I can't stop a grin from breaking through.

"Hasn't anyone ever helped you before?"

Deliah shifts.

"No," she grounds out.

Ah, that explains a lot.

"Well," I say, sliding one of her daggers from her belt, "usually, the one being helped shows some gratitude."

"I'm going to kill you."

I laugh again, pushing her scarf aside, and carefully slice her shirt to reveal the wound along her collarbone. Her cockiness is a good distraction from what she is. I focus on that.

"They also refrain from death threats."

"I—"

"Shh."

I'm almost sorry to cut off what was sure to be a beautiful threat judging by the glare she gives me, but now I need to concentrate. The wound begins on top of her shoulder and falls down, angled across her collarbone. It's deepest where it starts, which happens to be the place with the most muscles and tendons at risk.

"I hope you have some needle and thread in your bag," I murmur, "because I doubt I'll find any out there." I gesture vaguely around us.

"Of course," Deliah says breathily. "Rule number five; always be prepared."

I give her a quizzical frown but she shrugs, instantly wincing.

"I suppose that's a good rule," I say slowly.

I rummage through her bag, pulling changes of clothing, a small bundle of food, and the needle and thread free.

There's a clump of dried leaves hidden at the bottom, perfect for cleaning the wound. Aside from a thin notebook and pencil, she didn't bring much else.

"I need your scarf," I say, turning away from the bag's contents.

"No." Her voice is low, determined.

I shrug.

And tear the yellow shirt she wore that last day in town.

"Really? I liked that one!" she groans, lifting her head from the ground. Sweat pours down her face.

I cock an eyebrow. She's seriously upset about a shirt?

"I did ask for the scarf."

"Fine," she sighs, dropping her head as I press the wad of torn clothing to the wound. She grits her teeth but doesn't make a sound.

"We need a fire. Don't move."

"Yes, sir."

Dusk is in the air as I scour our little clearing for the tinder, kindle, and larger sticks that I'll need. It's not solely to boil water and make medicine with, we'll need a fire to keep warm for the night too. The clearing may be sheltered, but that won't protect us completely from the temperature drop once the sun disappears. I can't risk saving her life only to have her dying from exposure.

But away from her, I can no longer fight off my thoughts. I can't believe I'm helping her. Especially after what she did to me. But she's more than proved she could have killed me that day. So why would an assassin spare me, not once, but several times now?

There has to be a reason. A goal. A game. But it doesn't matter. She has what I need, which means I need to win her over, and helping her is my best shot. At the very least, I might be able to bargain with her. So I grit my teeth, and think of Zara.

I have the fire crackling within minutes, carefully loading dried wood to limit the smoke.

"What are you doing?" Deliah grabs my hand before I can add her medicinal leaves to a container of water.

"Making sure you don't die." I try to shrug free but her grip tightens, though her face pales.

"Then you'd better stop because I'll die of infection before the night's over."

I cock an eyebrow. "Perhaps the infection's already gone to your brain if you believe that." I gesture to the leaves, one of the most popular medicines for injuries. "These will help."

She rolls her stormy eyes. "Just be a good soldier and follow orders, OK? You need to make a poultice."

I blink at her.

"A poultice?" she says as though I've never heard the word before. "Much more effective."

"Fine," I shrug, tipping out most of the water. We'll do it her way. "Can I use them all?"

"Half now, half tomorrow."

I carefully add half the bundle, putting the rest aside.

I grab her knife from where I'd left it, turning it in my hand so the pommel is down.

"Whoa! What are you doing?"

I sigh heavily, stopping to give her a long look. Then I slowly use the knife to hammer the mix. "Saving your life."

"But my knife!" she yells, struggling to sit up.

I shove her back down.

"Well, I'm not using my swords. Besides, you don't need it with your magic."

"That's not the point," she grumbles, looking away.

I keep mixing the poultice, studying her as I work. There's something else there. Something else below that admission of never having been helped before. I can see it in the way she's so aware of every move I make. The way she tried to hide the stiffening of her muscles each time I reached for her knife. Each time I reached for her.

"Who hurt you?" I murmur. I don't know why I ask, why I care, but the words slip out.

Deliah gives me a strange look. "You were there."

"No," I say, shaking my head. "Not your body."

Her expression clears, and she turns away again. Deliah is quiet for so long that I don't expect her to respond. But, in that silence, I can hear a lot.

"Who hasn't?" she finally whispers, the flames dancing across her face as the memories dance in her eyes. A vulnerability, hidden deep inside.

She clearly wants to avoid talking about it, so I let the conversation go.

For now.

"Well," I say, "it's ready."

Before she can spit another wonderful comment, I peel back the makeshift bandage, and press a wad of the crushed leaves into the wound.

A pained grunt is the only sound that passes through her lips. I keep adding to it, keep pressing all along that line that trails from her shoulder down her collarbone.

Blood mixes with the juice of the poultice and trails across her tanned skin.

"So, where are you from? Clearly somewhere sunny," I say as I work, trying to fill the heavy silence that's descended.

She presses her lips together, but no sound escapes.

"What? No comments now?"

My words earn me another glare.

Done with the poultice, I sit back on my heels to give her a moment of space. Dusk is in the air, and after wiping my sticky hands clean, I add more wood to the fire. I don't have to leave her side, everything I need is already here beside me.

"Get the thread ready," Deliah orders, sweat now rolling off her.

I throw her a bemused glare and do as she says. Bossy, this one.

"Why are you doing this?" she asks, her breathing settling as the poultice does its work.

I grin lazily. "Can't walk away from a damsel in distress. It's a serious flaw of mine."

Instead of her mouth dropping open to argue as I'd anticipated, she simply studies me.

"No, I don't suppose you can, soldier. But that's not the real reason."

"No," I correct, admit, "it's not the *only* reason."

But I don't pursue it. Not now. Though this would be the best moment to hold it over her, I can't. I can't bring myself to do that to her, even if she deserves it. Besides, there'll be time later.

I gesture at her wound. "Ready?"

Deliah sucks in a deep breath. "Ready."

And just like that, I wipe the poultice away, its work done for now.

"Deliah—"

"Eilah," she cuts me off, holding my surprised gaze. "It's Eilah."

I blink. How many names does this girl have?

"Eilah," I say slowly, "I need to make sure there's no damage to the muscle or bone. This is going to hurt."

She rolls her eyes. "Obviously."

Clearly I don't need to waste careful words on her.

Sighing, I get to work. Rather than tug the skin together, I gently pull it apart. I'm not about to tell Del—Eilah this, but I've had rather limited experience working on injuries. If the muscle is damaged, I'm not sure what I can do for her. The thread I have can hardly stay inside her body.

One problem at a time.

"Are you all right there, soldier?" Eilah grunts between gasps. "Would you like another moment while I bleed out?"

"I'm working," I growl, not glancing away from her torn flesh that has indeed begun weeping again. "I can't see the bone, which is good."

A soft moan escapes her lips as I carefully move down the wound. It's deep, but there doesn't appear to be any serious damage. The cut overlaps with an old scar where it finishes on her chest. I try not to linger on it, but it was deep, jagged.

I release a sigh of relief. "Everything seems fine."

"Good," Eilah says, and I risk a glimpse of her face. She's as pale as a sheet, but her eyes are clear and bright. She's known her fair share of pain.

"Ready for the hard part, Eilah?"

She gives me a firm nod. "Just get it done."

Just think of Zara.

Carefully pinching her skin together, I press the needle through.

Her hand clenches at her side, and she forces out a deep breath.

"We'll start at the deepest part and work our way down."

"Uh huh," she grunts.

I continue the stitch, tugging lightly on the thread so it doesn't tear through her skin. I've done that before, and I'd rather avoid adding to her pain right now.

"So," I say, drawing out the word, "did you have the horse for long?"

Eilah huffs. "You don't need to distract me."

"What if I'm distracting myself?" I grin, eyes flickering to her face again before returning to her wound.

"I hope you're not. I'd hate for you to slip up."

"Hmm," I say, slowly pushing the needle through again. "You're right. We wouldn't want to leave you too marred."

Her lip twitches in the ghost of a smile, but it disappears as I pull her skin together. I wonder when the last time she genuinely smiled was. Not from spite or cockiness, but a true smile of joy. She's young, but something tells me her life has been this way for a long time. I shake the thought from my mind and continue down the cut, the wound growing shallower as I go.

I tug slightly too hard and her skin tears.

Eilah gasps, her hand latching onto mine.

"Sorry." I wince.

"I can't wait to kill you," she whispers. She glances at her hand still clutching mine and I swear a hint of red colours her cheeks before she lets go.

I grin and carefully continue.

"Good," I murmur. "Only a few more to go."

She says nothing, and I chance a glance at her face again, finding her eyes fixed on the stars winking into existence above us. I cock my head, feeling as though I've caught her off guard. Her energy has dimmed, the light in her eyes faded, but something alerts her to my gaze and her eyes snap to mine.

She raises her eyebrows.

I shake my head. "Making sure you're still alive. You've gone two minutes without insulting me. I was worried."

Eilah chuckles and I turn my face down to hide a smile at the soft sound. Then mentally reprimand myself.

"That can be remedied, soldier."

I can't help but reply. "I'm sure, but perhaps you should let me finish working first?"

"I suppose I can wait another minute or so."

"Great, that should give you plenty of time to think of something to say."

"I don't need to think about it. You're just too easy to insult, soldier."

"Oh, I think that still counts as an insult. You said you'd give me a few minutes." I grab her dagger from where it sat beside me. And cut the last of the thread away. "Good thing I'm done."

She blinks.

"Guess you needed that distraction after all." I grin, enjoying the way her face darkens.

"I—you—"

"I know, you're speechless," I say.

"I am not!" Eilah tries to rise but even more colour leaves her face.

"Whoa!" I say, grabbing her before she faints. "None of that. You need to rest."

"And I suppose you're going to take care of me tonight?" she asks, eyebrows rising. "Just going to forget everything between us?"

My stomach drops at the reminder.

But for Zara, I'll do it. I'd do anything.

I sigh. "For tonight."

She scoffs, shaking her head.

"Besides, I still need to make sure the rest of you is OK."

"I'm fine." She tries to pull away, and this time I raise my eyebrows at how weak she is.

"I'm sure you are. But I can't have you bleeding out on me because of some misplaced pride. Not when I still need you."

She sighs but says nothing so I take that as agreement.

Supporting her with one hand, I run my other down her back, carefully pushing and prodding, checking for internal and external injuries as I go. Eilah is silent while I work.

I check her other shoulder. Her muddied shirt has slipped backwards, from the cut I made on the front, and a brown mark peeks out from underneath. It doesn't quite look like blood in the flickering firelight, but I carefully lift her shirt away to be sure.

And suck in a quick breath.

A burn. A perfectly rounded burn that covers too precise of an area to be an accident.

No. That can't be right.

"Where did you get this?" I ask softly, forcing the words past my lips.

"What?" Her words are slurred.

"Eilah?" I pull back, stomach dropping.

Her eyes are closing, the whites showing. Her skin is slick. My eyes land on the scar on her chin.

That scar that made me think of an infant from so many years ago. A young girl who tripped on the front step of the Frigarth palace and hit her chin. That scar that felt like a co-incidence. Like nothing important. A trick of my imagination. But the burn ... I'd bet my life it's covering something. Perhaps the biggest secret Hera, Mother of Assassins, has ever kept. There's a birthmark under it. The almost perfect image of a flower.

"Eilah?" I ask, gently tapping her face despite my growing panic. "Stay with me."

But her form goes limp in my arms.

"Zara?"

15

Eilah

I TOLD HIM MY name.

I don't know why I did it. Why it suddenly felt important to hear it uttered from his lips as he stitched me back together in the darkness.

A moment of weakness. Of neediness. It won't happen again.

Except I've told myself that before. And here I am.

It *won't* happen again.

Daylight shines against my closed eyes, but I don't open them yet. I keep my breathing slow and steady, and listen for *him*.

He won't have left me. Not because he genuinely cares, but because of what I might know. I've been unconscious for hours, though. What was he doing for that time?

"I know you're awake ... Eilah."

The soldier's voice is gruff, hoarse. Even so, I allow my lips to turn up in a small smile.

"Can't a girl wish for the silence of sleep?" I open my eyes, wincing at the brightness of the morning sun. That telepath took more out of me than I thought.

I expect him to huff, but when silence greets me, I tilt my head, searching for him. Elvar's eyes are glued to me, but an almost faraway look lights them. As though he's seeing me, but not *me*. The coals of the dead fire sit between us, a lazy trail of smoke rising to the sky, coating the air with its familiar scent. He looks as though he hasn't slept a wink.

I cock an eyebrow, ignoring the stiffness in my body. "Did you receive a brain injury I don't know about, soldier?"

He shakes himself, running a hand through his short hair as he shoots me a frown.

"Your shoulder will be fine," he says after a long moment. I can't pin down this tone he's using. "It'll scar, but it won't be as bad as the one you left me."

So that's what's going on.

I huff, carefully pushing myself upright, resisting the urge to grimace at the pain that shoots down my shoulder. He thinks *that* was bad? He's lucky.

"That was nothing." I yank up my shirt, turning to show the thick, twisted scar running across my side, front to back. "I was down for a month."

The soldier stares unimpressed for a long moment, then slowly pulls up his own shirt.

I don't blink as the scar I'd left him with comes into view across his muscled abdomen. Healed. Someone healed him. The scar is gruesome, yet his skin is straight and flat, even so it's worse than I expected. But this isn't what he's showing me. He stands, turning to bare his toned back to the sunshine.

An arrow wound.

I scoff.

"You'll have to do better than that to top me," I say, laughter in my voice. I'm not sure when this became a game, but he lost before we even started. "There's a reason I always wear a scarf," I say as he lets his shirt drop back into place and turns to face me again.

A slight frown crinkles his brow as his eyes flicker to my neck. That slip in his mask is victory enough. But I want it all.

Grinning, I tug the fabric away with my good arm, baring the scar that should have been the end of me.

His jaw drops.

My smile widens.

"And that's why I didn't let you use my scarf last night. It's hard to go unnoticed with this showing. It rather screams trouble, don't you think?"

Elvar's eyes flicker between the scar and my eyes, disbelief shining in them as his face pales. Suddenly, victory doesn't taste as good.

"H-how?" He clears his throat, hoping to mask the strangled sound that's slipped in. I pretend not to notice, keep my smile cemented in place, and shrug.

"Mother wanted to make sure I could slit a throat properly." I pause, adding when the silence stretches, "She does it to everyone."

Or ... most of us. Nina hasn't had it done yet.

The thought turns my stomach.

Elvar swallows thickly, his eyes still glued to my neck. I tug the scarf back into place, wanting those haunted eyes to leave me alone now. When did that sadness overcome him? I didn't want to make him pity me.

"And the burn on your shoulder? How did you get that one?" he asks.

I cock my head. I guess he saw that one last night when he was checking me over. "I went places I shouldn't have as a child."

"Punishment?" Anger flares in his eyes.

"Accident."

But I can see the word doesn't convince him. Not after seeing what else Mother has done to me. I don't like this game anymore.

"How old are you?"

I let his words hang in the air. This isn't about his scars or mine anymore. This isn't about our past together. But I can't see what it is. And I hate being blind.

"How old?" he says firmly. Loudly.

My hackles rise, my magic swarms. But I push it away, put my hands out into the darkness to help me see, and say, "Nineteen."

His throat bobs again. "When did you join the assassins?"

"I don't think that's any of your concern, soldier," I growl. "What is this about?"

"Answer the question, assassin."

"Why? Why does it matter?" I gesture at him. "You're not as good at hiding your emotions as you might think. Your throat is thick, your hands have trembled twice now, and your eyes ... they're puppy dog eyes."

I *hate* those eyes.

He glares.

"Ok, they're not now. But they were. Big, blue puppy dog eyes." I purse my lips to stop the satisfied smirk breaking through at his lingering glower. He's easy to rile. "Why do you care?"

At his continued silence, I shake my head. "You know what? This has been nice, but I think I've overstayed my welcome." I look around for my bag, finding it next to him. I'm not about to get close to him, though. "I think I'll be on my way."

I haven't even finished pushing my feet under me when he clears his throat.

"You look exactly like them." His voice is ...

I freeze. Not knowing where this could be going. But an expression I have never seen before plays across his face, the intensity of his gaze holding me in place. My breath hitches.

"Who?"

"Laurel and Turin," he says quietly. "You even have that scar on your chin from when you tripped on the front step."

"I hit it on a chair leg," are the only words I can muster past the ringing in my ears, the throb of my blood. The magic calling to me, responding to the rage rising at the mention of my enemies.

"And that perfectly rounded burn sits right where you have a birthmark shaped as a flower. You were named after a flower." He stands.

"Stop."

"Zara."

16

Raiden

I FOUND HER. I actually found her. But somehow, she has no idea. No memory of the life that was stolen from her. And the things she's done, the things done to her ...

"Wait!"

Despite her wobbly legs, Zara is across the clearing before I can even stand.

"No. *No*. This has been nice, but I'm already behind on another job," she calls over her shoulder, her messy brown hair trailing down her back. Laurel's hair, longer, messier, but Laurel's.

Desperation swells and I grab her bag and my swords and hurry after her.

"Where are we going?" The words are through my lips before I've properly thought them through, but I don't take them back. For Zara.

"No"—she whirls—"I said 'I.' As in me. Just *me*."

Her words come as frost on the air, her eyes more blue than green. A quick glance at her uninjured arm shows ice crusted on her fingers. I know she must have immense control with the jobs she's pulled off, but I'd rather not test her at this moment.

I quickly swap tactics, crossing my arms and offering her a cocky grin. "You're still injured. And besides, you owe me now. I think I might come along and watch you work, assassin."

A muscle works in her jaw.

"Why? Want to help me?" She steps closer. "Do you want to be an assassin now, Elvar? Because I don't owe you anything other than letting you leave with your life. *Again.* I am not your lost princess and I don't know anything about her. I suggest you move on before I get sick of putting up with you."

I hold her icy gaze, ignore the glassy dagger slowly forming in her palm.

"It's my duty to protect you, Your Highness," I say quietly, feeling the truth in my bones, but she still flinches. "I go where you go. Your battle is my battle."

"And when my battle leads us against your home? What then?"

I still at the vehemence, at the truth in those words. I thought they had been a mere jab before, a way to keep me on my toes.

"You didn't think we were done with you, did you? After what you did," she whispers, even closer now, close enough that her words cool my skin. Ice whirls in her eyes.

"*We* did?" My fist clenches and I force it to release, force myself to ignore the now fully formed dagger resting against the scar under my shirt.

"Your people," she spits, "killed my family. My Aunt Lily. The greatest assassin in our compound."

"The Dragon Assassin?" I splutter, mind racing. "The one who came for Prince Gaara and Princess Cyra? You can't be serious! *She* killed your family."

Pain pricks in my abdomen, and I glance down to find blood dripping from her dagger. I meet her eyes again and this time it's not a smile of jest that lights her eyes. She slowly raises her hand, revealing a thick ring with a dragon crest. *Her* crest.

"Don't think for one moment that we've forgotten what was done. When I'm done with your precious king and queen, I'll be coming for Cyra of Ashennor. I'll finish what she started."

Cyra.

I take a deep breath and say nothing, knowing the only words I have would ruin any chance I have to stay with her, and stare down into those stormy eyes. The eyes of an assassin. The eyes of my princess.

"Fine," Zara says, withdrawing her knife, the tip flashing crimson before it melts. "Join me. Come and see what your *princess* really does."

There's an unspoken promise in those words. One that makes me certain there's more than one job she intends to finish before taking down Frigarth. Too bad she won't be doing any more jobs, other than the one she was born for.

17

Eilah

"**C**AN YOU WALK JUST a bit quieter, soldier?" I snap, as a twig breaks under his foot. I can't believe this. I don't care if he's quiet, *silence* is what I need if he's accompanying me.

A caw is his only response a moment later, and I watch the black figure of his shifted form flutter ahead.

"I'm not a princess, you idiot!" I shout after him.

I press a hand into my shoulder. The poultice he applied last night worked wonders, but now the wound aches. I sigh, closing my eyes. Why did I play that stupid game with Elvar? Right from the beginning, he wanted to ask about my burn. I can see that now. Part of me is impressed. Few people have played me so well, and it only worked because I was on the back foot right from the start. But the fact that he thinks I could be a princess ...

It's laughable.

I might spend a lot of time away from the compound and Mother, but my memories of her stretch back to early childhood, even a couple from when I was a toddler. I can even remember when I got the scar on my chin. And it wasn't on a step.

I'd told him as much, not that I needed to defend myself to him. There are no black spaces in my mind, no confused images or memories that don't make sense. No. I am my mother's daughter. And she is a queen, not of a country but of an entire continent.

But he's determined. I'm sure he's coming up with a reason for why I can't remember, why my memories don't match. It's sure to be ridiculous. Then I can laugh, and then I can kill him.

I stop, checking the position of the sun and altering my course to keep east, and my anger at the soldier fades to the background. Still smouldering, but not raging.

Aeris.

I hate her for what she's making me do.

An impatient caw snaps me from my thoughts.

"Shut it!" I yell, not sure if it's the rook or not. But I continue walking.

I should have known this day would come. She wasn't very good, anyway. A foolish girl with too many thoughts and emotions and *dreams*. It's a wonder she lasted so long.

The tall trees slowly thin, and I emerge into a rocky clearing. A grey boulder juts from the ground directly in front of me, and that's where the silk black rook lands.

He stays in that form, but cocks his head. His question is clear.

"None of your business."

I tromp past him. If he wants to come along, fine. But he doesn't need to know anything about what I'll be doing. And just let him *think* about stopping me.

It'll take a week to get to the coast and Aeris. Perhaps my injury slowed us down long enough that she'll have time to board a ship. If she's smart, she'll be gone before I arrive and her trail will be cold.

I'll be expected to follow, but Mother can't punish me if she's already gone.

We camp in the scraggily underbrush that slowly begins to take over the landscape, our bodies hidden more and more each night. No fire, and nothing more than foraged greens for dinners. We eat in silence. Though my shadow opens his mouth to talk several times, it always snaps shut when I shoot him a glare.

Conversation wasn't a part of this tentative deal that will be over the moment I'm done with Aeris. But it doesn't stop his eyes from studying me, locking on me every spare moment, his mind racing behind them. Princess. That's what those eyes say. Maybe I should pluck them out.

It's not until the sound of the waves crashing on the shoreline reaches our ears that Elvar breaks his silence.

"Why are we here?" he says, angling his body to face me.

I let my eyes trail over the bustling seaside town. The people of Hythemore are nomadic sailors, living on the seas until they need supplies. Then they come here for a glimpse of their rugged homeland.

"To kill my sister," I tell him, pushing past and heading straight for town. I just pray she's already on one of those many ships on the horizon. A trader maybe, or a cargo ship. Hidden somewhere below.

"Your … sister?"

I shake my head, hitch my bag higher on my back, and pick up the pace.

If Aeris is here, she'll have tried her best to hide her presence. It'll take someone who knows her well to find her. Thanks, Mother.

"Zara?"

"Don't call me that!" I whirl and Elvar nearly walks straight into me, barely managing to stop. "I am not your princess," I hiss, aware of how close we are to prying ears. "Make sure you stay out of my way, or you'll be joining my foolish sister at the bottom of the ocean. Understand?"

Elvar nods slowly, his steely eyes never leaving mine.

"Good."

I glance around and sigh. "She'll be there."

I point at the market stalls spread along the wooden docks. Aeris has jewellery to sell, supplies to buy, and a ship to book. It's the perfect place. She'll sell them over a couple of days, so no uncomfortable questions are asked.

"How do you know?"

"Common sense."

It's his turn to sigh as he follows after me, but I don't acknowledge his large form at my back. I merely straighten my spine and begin the search at the end of the markets and work my way up.

The salty air fills my lungs, the gulls call on the shore, and I can almost pretend I'm not here to kill her. I can almost pretend we're two normal sisters on our way to see if the legends of mermaids are true. I would have liked to find out.

The crowd grows thicker as I move along the stalls, a mix of the larger, burly people of Hythemore. Captains, most of them, with the occasional crew member collecting wares for a long trip. There's no other reason to be here. My eyes snag on a lithe, dark-skinned woman and I cock my head, taking in her flowing, dark blue clothing and the tattoos dotting her body. It's rare to see a traveller from another land, even here at such an important restocking point.

Dismissing the woman, I carefully avoid the many bodies, not wishing to make a scene yet. But there's no sign of Aeris. I can't help the spark of hope that grows the further I go without spotting her. She's not at the jeweller's stall, nor at the blacksmith's, none of the sea suppliers, and not at the various women's clothing stalls. Perhaps she made it out.

It's with a sick feeling in my chest that I spot my sister at the story weaver's tent.

"Wait here," I say to my shadow, but it comes out more of a whisper. I don't bother summoning any magic or reaching for my daggers. Now is not the time.

Aeris stands at the back of the small group crowded around the old woman, images floating on the air before her as a mix of colours. The weaver is perhaps the oldest fae I have ever seen, her skin sagging and leathery as though she were human, yet her eyes hold more knowledge than they could gain in a hundred lives.

My sister's once long, curly red hair is now short, dyed blonde though her roots are already shining through. She's literally cut ties with home. Aeris has abandoned her favourite weapon—a bow and quiver—for a small utility knife at her belt. I'm sure there are more knives hidden around her tunic and cloak. She can't be that foolish, can she?

I stop quietly beside her, eyes on the weaver as birds of lightning swirl around dragons. Mother told us this story once, and I find myself forgetting about my sister for a moment, captivated by the blues and reds that burst to life as the old woman weaves her tale.

"It was the mermaids, wasn't it?" Aeris says, her voice serene despite her death looming so close.

I wish she hadn't spoken, but I nod. "I knew you'd come here for them."

One night, one night of gushing about the stories she'd heard on a job, is all it took for me to find her. The light in her eyes had given her away. It's best never to love something. I'd already learnt my lesson by then. Now it's her turn.

"And I knew it'd be you she'd send," she says, finally turning to lock those brown eyes on me. She offers me a small smile, and in it I don't see an ounce of fear. "I'm glad it's you. You'll make it quick. Clean."

I clear my throat, returning my attention to the story playing out before us. Only two birds and one dragon are left. I don't know that I want to watch what happens next, but I don't want to look at Aeris either.

"Who's the soldier?"

"No one," I murmur. "Just a shadow I keep for the entertainment."

Aeris chuckles, light and musical, and a stab of pain hits my chest. I'll miss that sound.

"Have you seen any?" I say, turning to face her completely. Elvar's eyes are locked on me, over her shoulder, but I refuse to meet them and keep my face blank. "The mermaids?"

"No." She shrugs, but I can see the disappointment that stoops her shoulders. "The boat leaves tonight."

I swallow heavily, but how can I view her as a target when all I see is my sister? How can she be a traitor when those hands have killed to protect me? How can I cut that body when I've stitched it back together more times than I can count? How can I stop that beautiful tinkling laugh from ever sounding again?

I swallow again, and hide my shaking hands in my jacket.

"It would be a shame if you didn't get to see them."

I smile at the light that enters her eyes as they search mine, at the smile that tentatively raises her lips. I ignore the slight film that forms in my eyes, and I nod.

So there on the docks, we put our heads together, and catch up on all we've missed since we last saw each other three months ago.

18

Raiden

THE ASSASSIN IS SILENT as she rejoins me, leaving her sister behind and alive, and leads the way back into town. My eyes are glued to her, watching every movement, searching for any sign of her thoughts.

Zara doesn't say a word to me as she finds an inn, enclosed after the style of the humans to protect its occupants from the rough sea weather, and claims two single rooms. Her shoulders are taut as she clomps up the stairs, her hands still hidden inside her jacket.

I can't tell what she's thinking, what she's planning. Or when she'll do it.

She can't kill a babe, but can she kill a supposed sister? They'd seemed friendly on the docks, but that could have been a part of Zara's act. A trick to make the girl lower her defences.

She may be an assassin, but she's also my princess. That's the thought I repeated over and over as we travelled here to Hythemore, and that's the thought I keep repeating. Our past doesn't matter anymore. I won't hurt her, I won't kill her, but I can stop her.

Ideas to help the girl escape run through my mind as I follow behind the assassin. As soon as she's in her room, I'll need to leave, shift, and find the girl. Whisk her away before Zara knows. And then try to convince her it was the right choice.

It's not until the assassin's hand closes on the door handle to her room that I speak.

"What are you going to do?"

"None of your business," she snaps.

"Z—assassin," I say, keeping my voice quiet. Using her real name will raise her hackles, and I can't have that if I need to rescue her sister. There'll be plenty of time to reach the princess later.

She sighs, leaning her forehead against the door.

"I can't do it," she whispers as though it's a fault, a weakness. "I can't kill Aeris. But Mother ... it'll need to be convincing."

I can't help the grin that lights my face, the hope that rises in my chest at this little crack in her armour, in who she was raised to be.

I cross the short gap between us, place my hand over hers, ignoring the roughness of her scars, and push the heavy door open.

"Let me help."

The assassin's room is smaller than a cleaner's cupboard, with a small single cot shoved into the corner and barely a foot of walking space. No room for a chair. The window is covered by a dirty cloth. Mine, the room next door, will be the same. Instantly, I long for the outdoors, but at least the bed is clean and dry.

Zara scoffs and throws herself on the bed. "Biggest rooms, my butt."

I purse my lips to suppress a laugh and sit beside her, careful to leave some room between us. There might be a tentative truce, and I may be putting my own feelings aside, but I don't entirely trust her not to snap.

"What's Aeris's shifted form?" I ask when the silence lasts too long. I try not to read into it and what she must be thinking.

"A fox," she grunts. "Why? Want to kill a random fox and claim it's her?"

"No, I doubt Hera would believe that," I chide, repeating the words I'm sure are running through her mind. "But it would make it easier to smuggle her out."

She pushes herself upright, raking her hands through her long braid to free her brown hair. *I wonder how she fights with it so long,* I think distractedly.

"Yes, but I still need to *kill* her," she drawls.

"Stage it. Use some pigs' blood and swap out the bodies."

She stills, then flicks her hair over her shoulder, so long the tips brush the bed. "I thought you didn't want to kill anyone, soldier? You don't mind if I kill a random civilian to save Aeris?"

My eyes widen. "No, no, someone already dead."

Her eyebrows rise. "Do the king and queen know you steal dead bodies for fun?"

"I-I," I stutter. I did not think this through.

Her mouth twists into a smirk.

"Well, what's your plan?" I ask, a little defensively.

"I'll kill her on the docks in front of witnesses. The body will fall into the water. You can even pretend to arrest me, if you'd like." She throws me a satisfied smile, and I know she already had this worked out.

"What does Aeris think?"

"She thinks I'll need to be careful. Mother won't believe I'd kill her so openly and in front of people. But there are ways around that."

I frown. "How will she know the details?"

"Aside from when I tell her about it?" Zara scoffs. "She has people everywhere. She'll know about it before I get back."

Back.

She wants to go back to Hera. Panic surges in my chest.

I clear my throat. "Right."

I can't let her go back. I can't lose her again.

A series of sharp knocks on my door startles me awake, my body already sore in the cot. It's more comfortable sleeping on the open road than in this rickety bed.

"Soldier," Zara's voice hisses through the dim light of night.

I'm on my feet in an instant, a shirt halfway over my head when I tug open the door.

"What?"

I almost think I imagine the way her gaze locks on the scar she left me before my shirt falls into place. If I were human, I wouldn't be able to see her at all in the dark hallway, her body clad in black clothes, daggers in place at her hips. She meets my eyes with a fiery spark.

"It's time."

I blink. "What? Tonight?"

"Yes." She rolls her eyes.

I turn, snatching up my swords, irritation rising. "Why didn't you say that earlier?"

"Do I have to tell you everything, shadow?"

"Everything related to staging a murder, yes!" I can't believe she wants to do this now!

"Wait ten minutes, then come to the docks. Far end." She twists on her heel, leaving me standing in the doorway, staring after her.

"Right. The docks."

Eilah

I creep through the shadows like I was born to it, not noticing the cold of the night against my skin. A frozen heart, my mother always said. And that's why she sent me on this job. She knew I'd do it without any qualms.

I run through the plan again. Aeris will be up there in the shadows, waiting for the ship that is supposed to take her to safety.

This is perhaps the stupidest thing I have ever done. Rules one and two are definitely in danger tonight, not to mention five and six. And trusting that soldier to wait ten minutes is the icing on top of this disaster of a cake. But if it works, it'll be worth it.

I duck into the shadow of a large trader, the crew member pacing its deck with heavy steps completely unaware. The creaking of countless ships bobbing in the rising tide, their hulls rubbing against wood, will be enough to hide Elvar's footsteps as he follows me—the man can't walk silently to save a life—but it'll hide the presence of anyone else on the docks. I'll need to be careful.

I dart forwards, into the shadow of the next ship. The moon may be small tonight, but the night is clear and the stars shining, paired with the torches spaced at random intervals, the dock is bright tonight. I'm careful to keep my footing sure beneath me, one ill step could easily send me into the water. My stomach churns at the thought. I can swim, of course, but the mere thought of those waves closing over my head ... I shudder.

I stop two moors down from where Aeris told me she'd be hiding. The ship will be here any minute.

I peer into the darkness clumped around the ships, searching for any movement, a shadow darker than the rest, anything to give away my traitor sister's form. There! A dark shape against a mooring point tells me she's crouching. I shake my head. She just had to choose the ship that would take the far end of the dock to whisk her to safety. She should have chosen one further down, close to a building that she could hide in until the ship arrived. Or an alley that she could have run down in the event of ... me.

I shrug.

Maybe she knows it was inevitable.

A ship appears on the horizon, noticeable by the lantern on its keel, and that little shadow by the mooring pole shifts.

It's now or never.

I inhale deeply, pretend it's a nameless lord or lady I'm following, and reach for the magic. Feel the ice running through my veins, and pull it to the surface, forming a single, long dagger in my palm. For her, I'll make it quick.

"Aeris," I call, stepping out of the shadows, blocking her path to safety. It's me or the water now.

The shadow jerks.

"Eilah?" she says rising to her feet and stepping out into the open. "I was wondering when you'd come."

"I'm here."

The white of her eyes shine from under her hood as they flick to my dagger. "What are you doing?" her voice wobbles.

"My job."

"The guard will be here any second," she says, glancing over my shoulder.

"I'll be gone by then," I whisper, yet I know she can hear me above all the noise of the ships. "I'm sorry."

"I know." Her hand reaches inside her cloak, and I move.

Foot already forward in throwing position, I raise my dagger and shoot it towards her in one clean motion, pumping the force of my magic into it to speed it along. It hits her square in the chest.

A slight exhale leaves her body as she stumbles from the force of it. Her hood falls, revealing that bright curly hair, and my sister tumbles backwards. Into the sea.

I hear the splash as her body hits the water, and feel my shoulders drop.

"Halt!" the young voice trembles slightly. A boy. They put a boy on guard duty.

I close my eyes, summoning another dagger, praying I won't have to kill him.

But another, deeper voice barks out, "Don't move!"

About time, shadow.

"Drop the dagger!" he calls, closer now. He adds something quietly to the boy beside him.

I let the dagger dissolve, dripping onto the weather worn planks below me, ready to call it back in a moment.

Hurried footsteps sound behind me, as the boy sprints away, probably for reinforcements.

"Put your hands behind your back and stand still," Elvar calls, his voice hard. Angry.

I do as he says, a small smile tilting my lips unseen by him. His anger draws satisfaction from my very core.

His large hands grab mine, pulling them together as he wraps a length of cord tightly around them.

"What the hell was that?" he yells, yanking me around. His face is inches from mine, his chest heaving, and his eyes hard.

I tilt my head back, not that he's much taller than I am, and give him a smirk. "My job."

Pain flickers in his eyes and I barely keep the facade in place. This idiot actually thinks I killed her?

I cast a glance over his shoulder, no sign of the soldiers that boy has gone to fetch.

I draw closer to my shadow, my nose nearly brushing his. The salty air clings to him.

"Think we can get a move on?" I purr.

"W—" he frowns, his anger flickering in his confusion. "Now?"

"Right," he says slowly. He gives my arms a tug, and leads me away, down the docks and away from the sister that is swimming out to that ship. She'll climb aboard and hide until they are far out to sea.

Safe.

19

Eilah

"WHAT IS GOING ON?" Elvar says, shoving me roughly against a stone wall. I use the hands I've already freed to catch myself. His eyes narrow but he says nothing.

"I told you," I growl, pushing back my shoulders. "What do you think is going on?"

"I saw you throw a dagger at her!" he shouts, pointing in the direction of the docks we have long left behind.

I slap my hand over his mouth.

"You want to yell that a little louder, Elvar? In case you've forgotten, I just killed someone and they'll be searching for me and the soldier who led me away."

He shakes his head, tugging my hand away, his face hard. "What. Happened?"

I roll my eyes and summon another dagger to my hand.

He leaps forwards, grabbing my wrist, his other hand slamming into the wall behind me to catch himself.

"Calm down, you idiot. Look at it."

He stops, and finally notices what I'm trying to show him.

Elvar blinks. "It's blunt."

I laugh under my breath. "To say the least."

It's merely a long, rounded piece of ice, coming to a flat end nearly half an inch thick, a perfect replica of the one I threw at Aeris. "She'll have a nasty bruise, but nothing more."

I tug my hand free from his grip, and prod his chest with the dagger. "I know I'm a good actor, but you knew better."

He runs a hand over his short hair, letting out a long breath that seems to deflate him. "I'm sorry."

"Yes, well"—I cross my arms—"it's a good thing I was counting on you thinking I really did it. I doubt you can act that well."

"You—"

"Yes," I say, pushing him away, sick of him being so close. "You're an easy read, Elvar."

His mouth opens and closes again, I can practically see his brain whirling.

I raise an eyebrow.

"I'm sorry," he finally says again, ruefully. "I truly thought you wouldn't do it until the moment I saw her go over."

I shrug. "I don't care."

But it is fun to watch him squirm. To watch that bleeding heart control him.

"I do," he says, seriously, stepping close again. "I'm glad you saved her."

Something has changed in his eyes, and I glance away.

"Let's go. I'll get our stuff," I mutter.

"So, what now?" Elvar asks, a fire crackling between us.

I pause, but don't bother glancing up from my sketch-book. I haven't looked at him since the docks, now, we sit in the trees hours to the west of Hythemore. Dusk is in the air.

"We're going our separate ways." I continue drawing the eyes that I know are now glued to me. It's been a long time since I've drawn a person, and he is the only one around. Makes sense to draw him then. It has nothing to do with him being on my mind.

"You're not going to kill me?"

"I could, if you want me to." To be honest, I'm still not entirely sure I *shouldn't* kill him. He knows too much about me, and he seems to think he knows even more with this ridiculous princess theory.

He laughs, unaware of the tangent my thoughts have taken. The sound echoes in my mind, pleasant.

I keep drawing, keep pouring my attention into it. It helps me clear my head, and right now, there's a lot in it. Too much.

"What are you drawing?" His voice comes much closer than before, and somehow the blundering soldier has managed to catch me off guard. I snap the book closed, but too late, he saw.

"You have a real talent," Elvar murmurs, gazing down at me, firelight framing his strong form.

"Don't look at me like that!" I snap, standing merely to sit further away from him. Space. I need space. Or I might just admit to myself it's been nice having company.

"Like what?"

"Friendly. It's one step shy of love," I grunt.

"Is it?" he asks after a beat. "Is that a bad thing?"

He doesn't move, waiting for my answer.

"Love is for fools."

"I'm not a fool." He doesn't return to his seat but takes the place in the grass I vacated.

"I beg to differ," I scoff and deliberately ignore what his words could be taken to mean.

"Have you ever been in love?" he asks, voice gentle and curious.

OK, maybe I will kill him. I stare hard at him, chewing my lip. If it stops him staring at me with those stupid blue eyes ...

"I thought so once, but there's no such thing."

Elvar's face softens. "What happened?"

Fire flares in my veins. I don't want his pity. I don't want whatever this is that he thinks he's offering me. No. No. No.

"He's dead. He was my first kill outside of the compound," the partial truth rolls off my tongue easily, eagerly, as I wait for that face to wipe itself clean. A lie, because I can't let him know how weak Sorren made me. How much I had failed my mother and myself in that moment. That moment I couldn't do it.

He shifts in his seat, but his face remains calm.

"Did he do something?"

I open my sketchbook, flicking past Elvar's face, and start a new drawing. Keeping my hands busy, keeping my *mind* busy and the magic under control.

"He realized what I was," I say, carefully smudging one of the lines. "Something you can't seem to get in your head."

"Eilah," he says, and I wonder how hard it was for him to say my real name, to not project his lost princess on to me. "Tell me about it."

Maybe it's because I've never truly told anyone about Sorren—even Kyler—or maybe it's the desire to make him see me. But I tell him.

"I was on a long-term, deep undercover mission. I needed to infiltrate a family in order to get access to a group of men that came together only twice a year. We suspected the father in the family worked for them. And my way in was Sorren, his son." I keep drawing, adding line after line, swirl after swirl, something cathartic in the actions.

"Because it was a long-term undercover job, I—I had to let more of myself through. Lies are hard to maintain when there's so many of them. It was easier to keep up the facade of my fake life when I didn't have to pretend to have some stupid sunshine-y personality or something."

I chance a glance at Elvar at this and he offers me a nod, confirming he understands what I'm saying. That I had given a piece of myself to Sorren. That he had seen the real me, even if he hadn't known what had led me there, what my life really looked like.

"He quickly showed interest in me, and I guess it was nice," I swallow, but hurry on, brushing over the details that threaten to drown me. "We were together for a year before it was time to complete my mission, and he realized what I was."

"And he couldn't take it, soldier." I turn hard eyes on Elvar. "He tried to kill me, so I killed him."

I wonder if he can see the lie in my eyes. Because even then, even with my knife at Sorren's throat, my blood on the floor of his father's study, I couldn't kill him. I couldn't make myself take that life too. A life that had brought me joy.

I'd had Kyler do it weeks later.

It's something my clients can't grasp. I may be the one spilling the blood, but they're just as coated in it as I am.

I can't ever wash his blood from my skin.

Elvar is silent for a long time. "I have no delusions about what you are, Princess."

The charcoal of my pencil snaps, the end tearing the page.

"Do not call me that." How dare he. How dare he listen to all of that and call me his princess. How dare he.

"But it's what you are. You are a princess, and a warrior, and no matter how hard you try to bury your heart, it is still there underneath your rage and need for revenge." Elvar holds my gaze, a challenge echoing in his eyes.

"And you?" I spit back in his face. "We killed your princess. Don't tell me you wouldn't take revenge if you could."

"No." He shakes his head. "I want justice. That life was taken but not in the way you insist."

"If I was your princess, I would remember!" I say incredulously. "This is ridiculous!"

"Would you?" He jumps to his feet, words rushing from him. "Perhaps someone took those memories from you. What little you would have had at the time, Zara. Mind magic grows weak over time and distance, so the person would stay near you. Did you have regular check-ins during your deep cover?"

I did, but I'm not telling him that. Not when he would think that supports his point. Besides, it was perfectly normal to provide updates on the mission. We all do it.

"Surely there's someone in the compound who can do that," he continues, unaware of my silence.

"No! Are you kidding? A person with mind magic would be feared and respected above all."

Elvar pauses. "What's Hera's magic?"

"Nothing." I shake my head. "She doesn't have magic. My mother climbed her way to the top all by herself." Pride sounds in my voice.

"Don't go back to her."

"I won't." No use hiding it from him any longer. "I'm going to Frigarth."

20

Raiden

"I WON'T." ZARA'S EYES darken, and the assassin is looking out at me again. "I'm going to Frigarth."

I don't let her see the way those words hit me as she intended. But I wasn't lying when I said I have no delusions about what she is. An assassin is what she is, but now I know it isn't *who* she is.

"Good. I think it would be good for you to go there. Have you ever been? It might be beneficial for you to see the people you want to kill." I keep my voice light, as if we're talking about something trivial. Words are a game to her, after all. "You might find the loss of their only child was punishment enough—for a death they weren't involved in."

"Yeah?" She smirks.

"Not to mention the loss of Prince Gaara."

"I am so glad you thought I killed Aeris. You really cannot act." My princess rises to her feet, prowling towards me as though in her shifted form. "But come with me, Elvar. Come and see what I'm going to do to them."

I swallow heavily and shift gears, offering her a smirk. She responds to those.

"What you *think* you're going to do."

"Are you going to stop me?" Her head tilts, humour in her voice.

"Yes." I would, but she won't go through with it. Not when she sees King Turin and Queen Laurel.

"I'd like to see you try." She twists her fingers, icicles swirling between them, reflecting firelight. "Would you attack me with your pathetic swords? Or try to kill me in your bird form?" She chuckles.

"I wouldn't need weapons to stop you." I step closer to her, ignoring her words, and matching the look in her eyes.

"Oh?"

I drop the game.

"The babe," I whisper, and her eyes widen for a fraction of a second before she regains control. "Me." I reach for her hand again, flinching at the icy coldness, but the flakes whirling in her palm disappear. "Aeris."

There's one more name, one more name I could add, that I know deep down she regrets. But I don't say it, her pain going too deep and lasting too long.

Zara looks away.

"You're wrong," she mutters.

"No, I don't think I am."

"Have you forgotten Lord Dennel? Mivaan? Sorren?"

"No," I whisper, not correcting her on that last one. "I haven't. But now I'm starting to wonder if *you* ever will."

"I have a job to do." She wrenches her hand from mine, but this time I can see false bravado. The puzzle that is her and her games is slowly coming together, pages forming into something cohesive. "And I'm going to enjoy it."

"Just—just see them first." The words are through my lips before I can stop and think about them. But honesty is what works best, and I have a feeling she doesn't get much of it. "You don't have to meet them. But just see them. Please."

"I hope you're appreciated for your loyalty, Raiden." Her eyes study mine. It's the first time she's said my name. It's more distracting than I would like right now. "But it won't save them. I'll see them, and then I'll kill them. And I'll kill you if you get in my way."

"I'm prepared for that," I say. I won't let my princess kill them, no matter what it takes.

"Well, shall we go then?" she says, stepping back as though we've been discussing a pleasant trip to the beach.

"In the morning," I say, holding her eyes. *I won't leave you. I'm not abandoning you. Not again.* Even if it kills me.

Her eyes turn west towards Frigarth and the darkening sky. "Will you warn them?"

"No."

"Enough with the lies," she huffs, a tiredness entering her voice.

"I'll never lie to you. But if you want a truth, how about this one?" I can't stamp down the frustration that brews. I

147

should leave it alone, but I can't. She needs to know. To see. "That Gaara and Cyra were victims of your aunt and their families have been punished enough."

"Not this again," she sighs, kicking at a tuft of grass.

"That Cyra has suffered every day since, and your parents have suffered worse—with the death of Gaara, and never knowing if their daughter was dead or alive."

"We're going in circles." She crosses her arms.

"They've suffered enough," I say firmly.

"I'll be the judge of that," Zara says, eyes turning back towards Frigarth and Ashennor.

A plan is brewing in my mind as we begin the journey to Frigarth on foot. I have two possible chances to take, with two possible outcomes. And if I play it right, perhaps both will be at work at the same time.

I either need to unlock Zara's memories or have her see the pain of her parents and acknowledge that her job is done.

And what better way to unlock memories than in the exact place that they were made? But I need her to agree to go into the palace. To go in without the intent to kill.

It's a risk, but one I'll take if I can give my king and queen their daughter back. And give her peace.

But Zara is right. I can't act and that night with the scars was a fluke. Which means tricking her is not going to work.

"What?"

I jolt. "What?"

"You haven't said a word in twenty-two minutes. That's twenty-one minutes longer than you've ever managed," she says suspiciously, eye narrowing.

I laugh. "That's not true."

She throws me an unamused glare. "You haven't shut up about Frigarth and the king and queen since I decided I'm going there."

I shrug. "Now I'm just thinking about them."

"How long have you known them? You're rather attached. It's unhealthy," she mutters, veering to walk around a clump of trees.

"I've worked in the palace for most of my life, but I didn't work directly with your parents until you were taken. I've been with them ever since."

She's silent for a moment and I wait for her to deny who she is, but instead she says, "Seventeen years?"

"Yes." I peer at her from the corner of my eye, but her face is turned forwards, her expression unreadable.

"I thought you were older."

I frown. That is not what I was expecting. " ... No."

"Huh."

"I don't look that old!" I'm still in my first century. If I were human, they'd say I was in my early twenties. I hardly look older than Zara herself. And to the fae, appearance is usually all that matters.

I narrow my eyes at her, and the corner of her mouth twitches.

A full laugh bursts out of her. "I'm sorry. You're so easy to tease," she says around gasps for air.

All thought of offense is long gone at the sound of her laugh. I'm sure it's hard earned and rarely heard. And she just gave it to me. Instantly, I wish to hear it again.

"I'm sixty-four," I grumble. "You could be engaged to a prince my age."

"There are no princes your age."

"Ha, ha." But I'm grinning now.

The appearance of an age gap is somewhat unconventional, but ours is small. Smaller than the one between Cyra and I, and many thought we would make a good match. I shake the thought from my mind. This is not what I am supposed to be thinking about.

"There's a river up ahead," I say, unable to keep the happiness from my voice. Home, we're going home.

"There are rivers everywhere in this stupid country."

"Wait until you see the palace," I say. "Water—" I bite my tongue. "It's better if you see it in person."

I step ahead of her, altering our course slightly. "This way—there's a place we can swim across."

The rush of the river reaches our ears not twenty minutes later, and soon we break through the short reeds to arrive on its bank. My feet sink into the sticky mud instantly.

"Ready?" I say, unclipping my swords to keep them out of the water.

"Yep."

I turn at the slightly strangled word, and find her eyes glued to the crystal clear water, her hands gripping the straps of her backpack.

I glance between her and the river.

"Can you swim?"

"Of course I can swim," she barks, eyes flicking to me. "I just—I don't like it," she admits.

A princess of Frigarth and she hates water. More than that, a princess of Frigarth with ice magic and she hates water. I shake my head.

"It's not moving fast and it shouldn't be deep this time of year. You'll be able to keep your feet under you."

"Right," she clips.

"You can clearly see the bottom." The riverbed is covered in small grey and brown pebbles, not the most secure substrate, but at least she won't sink in it.

"Yep."

"Do you want—"

"You go first," she cuts me off, gesturing at the river she's yet to look away from.

"All right."

The bank isn't steep, and I'm on the edge in barely a step. With one glance behind me to check where the assassin is, I wade out into the river.

The water is crisp, refreshing in the warmth of spring as it rises up my legs and to my chest as I move out into the centre. Zara is an inch or two shorter than me—she'll be fine. She won't even have to swim.

Arms over my head to keep my swords dry, I check behind me again.

Zara is barely a meter in, the water at her knees, pace as slow as she could go.

"Come on," I call.

She shoots me a glare and I swear the temperature of the water drops by several degrees. I suppose I should be grateful she didn't freeze it with me still in it. Progress.

"That's only going to make you more miserable," I call over my shoulder and continue on.

The assassin grumbles something in response that I don't hear, but I don't bother calling back to her. Soon the water lowers, my wet shirt clinging to my skin.

A gasp and a splash sound from behind me.

"Zara?" I whip around, and she's gone.

Throwing my swords blindly at the bank, I leap after her.

The water isn't fast, but she's moving away from me with the current. The water isn't deep, but she can't get her feet beneath her. And it's all because of that thing on her face that I won't ever call her out on. Because it might be the death of me.

Panic.

As her head bobs above the water, I grab a fistful of her shirt and pull her towards me.

"It's all right," I say over her gasping and spluttering, water splashing in my face as her arms flail. "You're OK."

She latches onto me, long hair sticking to her face, wet cheek pressed to my jaw. One of her legs snakes around mine.

"Stand up," I say gently, keeping a firm hold on her body. My hand is pressed hard against that twisted scar on her side she'd shown me, but I don't shift my grip. "Put your feet down."

"I can't," she splutters, her grip tightening. It would almost be funny, if I didn't know how many people have died in water they could stand in.

"Yes, you can. The water's barely past my chest here."

I can feel the moment her feet touch the ground, and her body steadies, but I don't move. She pulls back a little, enough that I can see the panic is starting to leave her eyes.

"See?"

Her fist thumps hard against my chest, but the other one stays firmly latched to me.

"OK?"

She nods, water dripping from her chin.

"Come on, then," I say, dragging her with me towards the opposite bank. This close to her, the sweet scent of her clings distractively to my nose.

Her feet stumble in the mud and my grip tightens, keeping her close. I don't release her until we're clear of the riverbank, but Zara doesn't jump away from me as I expected. Doesn't brush off my touch.

She simply stares with rounded eyes, her cockiness completely gone.

"I'd better find my swords," I say, offering her the chance to collect herself. My arms feel empty as I pull away.

Zara nods gratefully.

I hear her moving around as I belt my swords back into place.

"We should move. I want to get over the other one before dusk."

"Other one?"

I give her one of her own customary glares, not acknowledging what happened as she wishes.

"We're in Frigarth, Zara."

She glares back, wringing out the new shirt she'd bought in Hythemore as she does. Back to her old self then, as expected.

21

Raiden

THE FRIGARTH PALACE APPEARS on the horizon early in the morning two days later. Its starlight exterior is simple and unassuming in the light of day, and something within me eases, even as my nerves rise. Home. But not safe, not yet.

Zara's eyes glint in the early dawn, and I try to ignore the way her stormy eyes are brought out by the early morning fog. It'll be a hot day, once the fog clears.

"Eilah," I say, trying to keep the urgency out of my voice.

"Eilah, now, is it?"

I nod, refusing to meet her tone. "I'm calling in the two favours you owe me."

Her face darkens.

"Two?"

"Yes. I've saved your life twice."

Ice appears on her hands. "If you think that will stop me from killing the king and queen, you are sorely mistaken."

I shake my head. "No, but I want you to do something for me."

"What?"

The ice doesn't disappear. In fact, it spreads up her arms.

"Give me a day. One day." I hold up a finger.

The assassin doesn't say a word, so I take that as permission to continue.

"You've never been here before, have you?"

"Not the capital," she admits, eyes narrowed.

"Walk through the city, see the people, and then, then see *them*."

An amused smile twists her lips. "You're going to take their assassin straight to them?"

"Today, you're just Eilah. I'll show you Zara's old room, and you can see her parents from a distance. You said you'd be the judge of their suffering. I'm giving you the chance to see it."

Zara bites her lip and the ice slowly recedes down her arms, disappearing when it reaches her fingertips.

"Fine," she grunts. "But then my debt to you is clear, and I'm back to my job tomorrow."

I swallow heavily, all my hopes on this one chance.

"Agreed."

Zara has no clothes other than the dark outfit she wore to

fake Aeris death, the fundraiser dress, and the dark dress she wears now since I ruined her yellow shirt. There's no chance of anyone recognizing her as the princess, but if Hera truly has eyes everywhere, she can't walk into the city as herself, either.

"Better," I say, scanning her from head to toe. Her long hair is tied high, hidden under a wide-brimmed hat. Her lean form is covered by a baggy shirt and oversized overalls. A neckerchief sits at her neck, and her daggers—that I've never seen her use—are buried somewhere among her clothes.

"I look like a farmer," she says flatly.

I stifle a grin, leaning against a bumpy tree trunk.

"Oh! Nearly forgot." I hand her a pair of wide-framed glasses.

"This is the worst disguise I have ever worn."

I frown. "But it'll work, right?"

She shrugs. "Maybe."

"Perhaps you should chew on a piece of grass?" I suggest, somehow keeping a straight face.

Zara scowls.

"And what about you? What are you going to wear?"

"What do you mean?" I say, glancing at my simple shirt and pants, my swords at my hip.

"Aren't you a bit obvious?"

"I live here," I say, pointedly.

Her scowl deepens. "Let's just get this over with."

I sling her bag over my shoulder and set off back into the city. Though we've travelled from the west, I led Zara around to the far eastern side of the city. Frigarth is divided into two by a fae-made wide river to provide water for crops. It means the outer side of Frigarth is vastly different from the side closest to the palace. Both are beautiful in their own right, and I want her to see it all. To experience her country in the way she should have already.

Houses are dotted more haphazardly here, each one open in the fae custom, even the human homes. It's in stark contrast to the Conquered Lands, where the people hide inside homes that mark them as human. As targets.

Zara's eyes scan side to side as we walk, easily keeping pace beside me. As we draw further in, the fields come into view. Plots and plots of kilan berries, their thin stalks twisting around stakes and wire frames, leaves shining in the sun. The wind kicks up their sweet scent, mixed with the fresh earth wrapped around their roots.

"This farm was new when I was born. It was started by a human family fleeing Ashennor. Now it's the biggest in the kingdom. Thanks to Gaara."

She says nothing, her eyes lingering on the plump golden berries glinting in the daylight. An older man walks among the plots, stopping to scan each and every plant he passes. A man and his young son follow along behind him.

"That'll be Jacob," I say, waving to the old man. "The owner. His grandfather started the farm."

"Hmm."

Soon we're surrounded by plots of every vegetable, berry, and fruit that will grow here. Human and fae work the lands. The buzzing of insects fills the air, and birds sing from the trees. I never grow tired of the walk home.

But a glance Zara's way reminds me not to lower my guard. Her eyes are back on the palace, scrutinizing every detail.

"You're not working today, assassin," I murmur. "So, stop looking at the palace like you're planning to siege it."

"Maybe I am," she says, smiling coyly, but that glint disappears from her eyes and she returns to studying our surroundings.

The steady flow of the river sounds above the low murmur of conversation, and more fae and humans begin to line the streets, moving to and from the inner city. They walk together, talk together, laugh together in a way no other country is yet to match.

Zara changes direction, and I eye her path to the small wooden bridge sprawled across the river.

"Not that one," I call after her. "We'll go further up to the main one."

She throws it a puzzled glance over her shoulder but follows after me. If she thinks that's our main bridge, she's got a surprise coming.

The starlight bridge is busy this time of day, but it's a sight the princess can't miss. I pretend not to notice the way her footsteps catch when she finally sees it.

Sprawled across the river, the starlight bridge—the rare stone white in the daylight—stands out against the green backdrop of the crops. Patterns of vines, leaves, birds, and butterflies swirl across the railings, carved deep and painted with starlight flecked reds, greens, blues and yellows. It is truly a sight to behold, especially at night.

The stone bridge is crowded with people on foot and horse, pulling or driving carts full of produce and fabrics. We join the bustle, carefully making our way across the gentle flowing river. Fish leap from the waters, swimming in and out from under the bushes overhanging the banks.

A fae soldier ahead catches my eye, his own lighting, and nods. "Sir."

"Nox."

Zara watches him pass, her head tilted down to hide her face under the brim of her hat, but then her eyes catch on something else, darting between objects and people. Lingering on the mechanisms we use to keep the water table below the city in check.

Without that mind calculating behind dark eyes, it's the most alive she's ever looked.

And that knot inside my chest eases marginally.

But it tightens again once we're on the other side of the river and the palace stands over us. I cast a glance her way, desperately hoping I can trust her to hold to her word to give me this one day. One day to show her the truth.

22

Eilah

THE PALACE LOOMS OVER us, the starlight glinting under the shadow of a large cloud, and I can't draw my eyes away from it. I've never been so close to them before. So close to the targets I've been preparing to take out for my entire life. Checking off kills like a game as I slowly draw closer to that final level. But they'll have to wait one more day.

I pretend not to notice Elvar's glances, the worry he thinks he's hiding behind a blank exterior. But assassins are trained to read even the little changes in body language. And he is an open book.

"Relax," I say, starting up the path to the palace. "You'll have your day."

"Good," he says, but his callused hand grabs mine. I let him stop me but turn narrowed eyes on our joined hands. "But we're not going up yet."

I raise my brows. "Not chickening out of our deal, are you?"

"No, there's some food we need to try first." His eyes light up and a surprised laugh escapes me. I pretend not to notice the way his eyes linger on my mouth.

"Food?"

"There's a bakery down the road," he points to our left, "they sell this amazing vanilla bean cake."

I stare at him, seeing a totally different side of my shadow. "Is this love, I hear?"

He starts to shake his head, then stops and nods, grinning.

"You'll see."

"Can I have my hand back then, soldier?"

"And if I said no?" he says, quirking an eyebrow.

I step into him, meeting his eyes. Those blue eyes that drink in the sight of me.

A small grin tilts his lips, almost a smirk.

"Then I'd have to cut yours off," I purr.

"Fair enough."

He abruptly drops my hand, pivots on his heel and heads off down the street, stepping over a small water channel in the pathway as though it wasn't there.

If it wasn't for the way his shoulders are a bit stiffer than usual, I might think he actually trusts me to follow.

But I do, not bothering to look back at the palace. Elvar might have his day, but I'll have mine.

Mother might even be impressed I've accomplished it without her knowing. Her face will be something to behold when I tell her.

The soldier leads me down the stone path, easily weaving through the crowds despite his broad frame. Many of them seem to know him. He returns their smiles, politely nodding, but it's clear he's uncomfortable by the recognition. Interesting.

"Here," he says, stopping in front of a small building with a water fountain out the front. It's the thirteenth I've seen since entering this water-filled city. Apparently, they use decorations, channels and pipes to stop the place from flooding. Makes sense, I guess. But I would have not built a city here. Problem solved.

A sweet mixture of cinnamon, honey, and orange wafts out into the street, followed by the comforting smell of warm bread. Breakfast duty was always the short straw in the compound, but it did mean I could have the first bite of fresh bread. Or the first loaf if I could fight off whichever sibling was baking with me.

My mouth waters.

"There's barely anyone in there," I say sceptically, but my feet move forwards of their own accord.

"Guin's bread sells out fast in the morning, but her vanilla bean cake is a city secret." He casts a searching glance for the sun. "It should be ready by now."

The front of the shop is open, of course, and stepping inside is almost a continuation of the street. But filled to the brim with nearly empty shelves. It's an odd conflict for such a packed shop, but the crumbs and flour left behind shows that the shelves were indeed full this morning.

"Guin?" Elvar calls, scanning the racks.

A head pops up from behind a counter and I barely suppress the startle.

She's a small woman, thin and lean despite the usual stereotype of bakers. Her hair is long, greying and tied away from her face, revealing pointed ears. She must be ancient.

"Raiden? Where have you been? It's been weeks!" she chides.

"Sorry, Guin," he says sheepishly.

"I suppose you're here for the vanilla bean cake?"

I purse my lips, hiding the smile that threatens to break through at this new discovery about my shadow. He likes food. Loves it, if this woman's knowing expression and his sparkling eyes are anything to go on. Who would have thought it?

Perhaps I could poison his food one day. I frown, shoving the intrusive thought away. That's for another time.

He nods. "Is it ready?"

"Just about," she tuts. "Grab a table."

I take the lead, aiming for a table with a good view of the street and the building to our right, where customers wander between aisles of stone and wooden homeware.

Elvar sighs but follows, taking the seat beside me.

"Who's this?" Guin says, openly scanning me with crinkled eyes.

"His cousin. Twice removed," I say, bluntly returning her studying. Weathered hands, wrinkled face, but clean and somewhat nice clothing.

She smirks. "I doubt that, honey. Relatives don't gaze at each other the way you two do."

Elvar coughs, his hand shooting out to grip my icy fingers under the table. "Is the cake ready now, Guin?"

"No."

"Then perhaps we could have some kilan?"

She gives him a shrewd look. "Don't think I can't see what you're doing, young man." But she disappears behind the near empty racks.

"Don't kill her," Elvar whispers, low enough that Guin's fae ears won't hear.

I say nothing, seething.

He squeezes my hand. "Eilah."

"Fine!" I yank free of his grip. "But there were no looks! Unless you count the one where I was planning how to poison you."

He smirks. "Sure."

"I said I wouldn't kill her; you I haven't decided."

He quietens, but that smirk stays firmly on his smug little face.

We sit in silence until Guin returns with two glasses of golden liquid balanced in one hand. Kilan.

"Here," she says, roughly plopping the glasses on the table. "For the record, you're a beautiful couple."

I'm halfway from my chair before Elvar's iron grip pulls me down.

"Thank you, Guin. Perhaps that nose could go sniff out that cake now?"

"You two are no fun!" the woman scowls, throwing her hands up. "But I think it should be ready."

"Go," I growl, between gritted teeth.

"All right, no need to be so grouchy."

Guin potters off, disappearing around the racks again. A soft laugh carries out to us.

"What?" I throw at Elvar, sensing his eyes glued to me.

"She doesn't mean any harm."

"So, I should excuse it when she causes it?"

He tilts his head. "No, but killing isn't always the answer."

"I wasn't going to kill her!" I hiss. "Maybe she'd lose a finger, or that giant nose that keeps finding itself in places it shouldn't, but she'd be alive when I'm finished with her!"

His lip twitches, but the smile doesn't break free. "You didn't deny it, though."

I still, eyes narrowing yet again. "Be very careful with your next words, Elvar."

"You didn't deny when she called you out as not my relative. That's all I was going to say."

"Well," I say, keeping my glare locked on him, "she wasn't wrong."

"No, she wasn't." He releases his hold on me, and I pretend not to notice the strange emptiness that follows. My mind reels. There most definitely weren't any looks between us. At least not on my part. I can't afford to let my guard down again. Not when Sorren …

New rule—not that it should have to be a rule but sometimes common sense loses—keep men at a distance.

Stupid woman.

Guin reappears several minutes later, carrying two plates, each with a large slice of cake.

"The icing hasn't finished setting, but I'm sure you won't mind." She places the cake down and accepts some coin from Elvar. "Give me a yell if a customer comes in."

And she vanishes again. She must have an oven behind the racks that I can't see. Whatever, I'm just glad she's gone.

"If you don't hurry up, I'll eat yours too."

Elvar has eaten half of his cake, while I've been staring after the woman.

I shrug, gripping my fork. "Try it." But I turn my eyes to the cake before me, and my mouth instantly waters again.

It's a three-layered white cake, with vanilla icing between each layer and decorating the top. White chocolate chips cover the cake.

I've never had anything like it.

The first mouthful is pure sweetness, the second is bliss.

Though she's a terrible, nosy old woman, Guin's cakes *are* something.

"Think you can forgive her now?" Elvar asks, scraping up the left over icing on his plate.

"I'll consider it," I say around a mouthful, another already on its way to my mouth.

Cake finished in barely three minutes, I wash it down with the kilan, and turn to Elvar with a grin. "I see your plan now."

"What?"

I pause, questioning myself, questioning if it breaks the rule I'd made seconds ago, but continue on. "You intend to make me too full to fight, so I'll have to wait for tomorrow."

"Hmm," he says, "I hadn't thought of that. But now that you mention it ... Guin!"

"No! Don't call the old bag back!" I grab his huge arm and yank him from his chair, hurrying from the building.

"Where ne—" I start to say, but my eye catches the glint of sunlight on metal. "Oh!"

"What?" Elvar calls, a step behind me as I beeline to a shop bustling with women.

"Look!" I gasp, picking up the two pencils, their make noticeable by the silver leaf on the end that had caught the light. "I've been searching everywhere for these!"

I clutch them tightly, admiring the care gone into them. The lead is smooth yet solid. I bet they're a dream to use. I carefully position one in my grip as though I'm going to draw, and a soft chuckle leaves me.

Elvar is silent and I glance up to find his eyes fixed on me.

"That look is back," I warn, telling myself I don't enjoy it or him.

"Sorry." He clears his throat. "You should buy them."

"Hmm." I stare down at the pencils unseeingly, mentally calculating how much coin I have left. I won't have enough left to get home if I buy these. I should have set out with more. Or demanded extra from Lord Langford, come to think of it.

My shoulders droop. "I don't have enough."

"Good thing I do," Elvar says. His hand closes around the pencils and before I can say a word, he marches inside.

"Raiden?" I squeak, hurrying after him, but he doesn't hear me, already talking with the owner. The man must have run.

"I'd appreciate it if you wait a week or two before charging them," he says to the man. "They don't know who it's for yet."

"All right," the man draws the word out, clearly unsure.

"Don't worry, Her Majesty would have my head, not yours." He claps his hand on the man's shoulder. When he turns, his eyes land on me and he gives a sheepish grin. My heart stutters.

"I may have only paid half."

My mouth drops open and he squints an eye, waiting for me to rip his head off, but all that comes out is one loud, long laugh.

The king and queen bought me two sketching pencils. Or one—if Elvar truly paid half.

"I'll be sure to thank them right before I do the job!" I laugh.

He frowns but says nothing, handing me the pencils.

"You are too good, Elvar," I chuckle, but despite the ridiculousness of him charging the people I'm going to kill, my heart warms a little. I tuck the pencils away inside my overalls.

"Right. Where were we going?"

"The palace."

That wipes the smile straight from my face.

The palace of Frigarth is obnoxiously beautiful. I kind of like it. Not that I'll admit that to Elvar. I'm sure he'd take any sign of approval as admittance to being his long lost, dearly loved princess. Eugh.

It's long and sprawling, going out rather than up. Even from a distance, I can see water pouring down the front step.

"Is that"—I frown, peering closer—"coming from *under* the palace?"

My shadow grins. "It is. There's a spring behind the building that travels underneath and lets out across nearly fifteen meters of the palace."

"Definitely obnoxious," I mutter, starting forwards.

"What was that?"

"Nothing," I quip.

He stops. "It's not obnoxious."

"Guess you did hear me then. Can we hurry up and get this over with? I would rather be inside the not obnoxious palace before nightfall."

He shakes his head. "Fine, let me lead the way."

I sweep my arm forwards dramatically in a gesture to tell him to take the lead.

He moves past me, then stops. "No daggers."

"Cross my heart, soldier. No daggers."

"Or anything else," he says, looking down at me.

"I gave you one day, Elvar. But you're wasting it."

I follow after him, finally stepping into the shadow of the palace, ignoring the way he continues shaking his head.

"Elvar?"

My head snaps up and I mentally berate myself for getting distracted with my soldier and not focusing on my surroundings.

"Hada! It's good to see you."

I keep my face carefully blank as he steps forwards to shake the woman's hand. She has shoulder length, brown hair and wide brown eyes to match. A sword is at her hip, and a wide smile lights up her face.

I study their interaction closely, but there's nothing too friendly between them. Nothing *more*.

"We didn't expect to see you back so soon."

"Just a quick check in," Elvar says, glancing over his shoulder at me. "Would you have a message sent to the king and queen for me?"

Hada follows his gaze to me, a puzzled frown crossing her face. "Sure."

"Thanks," he says. "I need to get my friend settled before I see them. Let them know I'll need to see them in the ballroom in half an hour."

"Of course! It's good to have you back." She claps him on the shoulder and runs ahead of us, taking the step with ease, not stopping, as though the little waterfall on the step in totally normal.

"Does everyone know you here, Elvar?"

"Mostly." He shrugs. "I've been here a while, remember?"

"Yes, yes, you're old. I know."

"Come on," he growls, "I want to show you your room."

23

Eilah

R AIDEN LEADS ME THROUGH the palace as though he could walk through it blind. He probably could, and it makes me view him differently. I think back over everything he's said about his job, his place here, and the royals.

"You're important here," I say, a statement more than a question, as I rip my eyes away from the water flowing underneath the clear flooring. My bare feet are cold against it, but the feeling isn't altogether uncomfortable.

"Yes," he says, not looking over his shoulder.

"How long have you been searching for the princess?"

He's silent for a long moment, some inner war waging inside him that I can't guess at. He's never been quiet about her before. So why now?

"Ever since she was taken."

Ah.

"And you've reported directly to the king and queen?"

"Yes." His shoulders are tight. He's waiting for me to say something mean, or perhaps he's wondering what information it is I'm probing for.

"So ..." I say, deciding to tease him, "if I killed you, it would upset them?"

He whirls around, eyes narrowed.

I give him an innocent look.

"Just wondering. Besides ..." I trail off, looking over his shoulder. "Is that it?"

Elvar's gaze searches me as I stare at Princess Zara's room. "Yes."

"Let's get it over with," I say.

I know what he's trying to do, why he's staring at me so intently.

He thinks I'll remember this room. This place that holds the last memories of a child. But I won't. I was never here. Never as a princess, not even as an assassin. But I keep my face blank. Not a flicker of emotion is allowed to cross it so long as Elvar studies me. He'll take it as a sign.

Which might not necessarily be a bad thing if it gets me face-to-face with the royals, but it would be messy. And I don't do messy.

"You go ahead."

I give him a pointed glare, but he doesn't budge.

"Fine."

I push through the transparent curtain across the entranceway, finding a young girl's room in perfect condition. As though the child is playing in another room, not lying dead somewhere these seventeen years.

The room is walled, unlike most fae rooms, with windows overlooking the city in the far wall. They were careful with the girl. Despite, or perhaps because of, the walls, the room is large and spacious.

There's blood on the floor.

I stop, staring down at the large rust-coloured patch.

"That's mine," Elvar whispers from the entranceway.

I glance over my shoulder at him, at the ghosts that stare back from his eyes.

"Yours?"

I'd thought it was the girl's.

He nods.

And now it makes sense why he's searched so long. He was close, so very close to saving her.

"You need to forgive yourself," I murmur. "There's no stopping us."

I chose my words carefully, reminding him of what I am and where I belong, but still to bring comfort. I don't know why that matters. But it does in that moment, as I stare down at the blood and picture the scars he'd shown me. None of the marks on his body suit this stain. It must have been a skilled healer, and a kind one not to have left a scar behind.

But then, Mother is the one who insists our healers leave a mark behind. To wear as a trophy or a punishment.

I shake the thought from my mind and cross to the small cot in the corner, inspecting the blankets roughly tossed aside. The realisation strikes me. This room hasn't been touched since the girl was taken. The room is heavy with sorrow and love.

I've never seen anything like it.

I shove at the heaviness sinking into my chest, stroking that anger back to life. *Good*, I think, furiously. *They deserved this. They never truly knew their daughter, as I never knew my aunt.*

My finger absently traces the outline of a waterfall on the cot as I study the toy hanging over it. A niggle of *something* sits in my gut as it turns. A seadragon and mermaid floating past. I think I've seen one of these before, perhaps in one of the seaside cities. I latch onto that thought, determined not to feel sorry for these people. If they bought from a shop, then it was cheap, a mere trinket. Nothing spectacular for their princess.

Shrugging, I turn away, eyes roaming over the shelves lined with books and toys.

"You people really like water," I say, crossing to study a wooden carving of a waterbuck. Unusual, but it's rather beautiful.

A swan sits beside it, and I draw back. Remembering the details of my aunt's last mission. How she'd trapped a princess in her swan form in order to take her place and infiltrate Frigarth's royal family. She'd even been inside this palace.

I huff, flicking the toy with a finger.

Elvar shifts behind me but remains silent.

"All right." I clear my throat, not liking how quiet I sound. "Shall we go see them?"

I turn to find Elvar closer, only meters away now, those blue eyes sweeping the room before landing on me again. I pretend not to notice the way his strong shoulders drop minutely, the slight crinkle that settles between his brows.

I pretend not to notice how my heart twinges.

"I'm meeting them in the ballroom, but there's a spot you'll be able to see them from." He steps closer. "Remember our deal, Princess," he whispers.

I grin, baring my teeth. "Keep calling me 'princess,' and I won't."

"OK, assassin," he draws the word out, closing the distance between us, "but I'll hold you to that."

"I'd like to see you try."

His eyes darken. A muscle twitches in his jaw.

"But a promise is a promise. I won't touch them, for now."

Elvar lingers, the space between us smaller than I would desire. And yet still too wide.

Remember the new rule. Remember the new rule.

His lip twitches as though he can read my thoughts.

"We'd better go, or we'll be late."

Elvar leaves me in a tight little alcove in the small sitting room beside the ballroom. I can see straight into the room, my view unobstructed, yet no one would see me here unless they stood directly in front of me. Hidden inside of a supporting pillar, it's a perfect place to hide, or spy from. Curious.

My shadow strides into the magnificent ballroom, his back straight, and his gaze fixed firmly in front of him. He won't give away my position. But is that for me, or out of concern for our deal?

"Raiden?" a soft voice calls, and a moment later a woman with long, greying-brown hair hurries inside, her eyes fixed on him. Laurel is a tall woman. Her frame would be strong if not for the way that sorrow has aged her. I know instantly that's what it is. Because a fae of her age would not have grey in her hair, or wrinkles forming on her face. Her posture would be lighter, her eyes brighter.

Satisfaction and guilt rage in my chest.

"My queen," Elvar says, bowing only slightly. As if he's been berated for bowing before yet can't stop. Typical of him.

Laurel grabs his hands, but before she can say anything a man enters the room.

I cock my head as I take in his large frame. He's a strong man, and yet ... the same sorrow hangs over him as his wife. Turin.

My father is unknown to me, a man Mother met on a mission. Unknowing or uncaring, he's never met me. Turin's sorrow ...

"Raiden," he says, his voice deep, and a thrill of something unnameable rushes through me. I find myself hanging onto his words, the sounds rumbling from him. "Are you well? We did not expect you back so soon."

Laurel glances back at her husband, taking his large hand in hers as he stops beside her. A question is clear on their faces, and yet they can't seem to ask it.

Raiden merely shakes his head.

"I was in the area and wanted to check in."

The king and queen try to hide their disappointment, but I can see it from here. Seventeen years and they still hope for news.

They've suffered enough. Raiden's voice, his insistence, echoes in my mind. *They've suffered enough.*

Hope is the worst kind of torture. They've lived with it all these years and here they are, still clinging to it. Still letting it control them, letting it raise their spirits only to bring them crashing back down.

Maybe ... maybe this is enough.

Elvar clears his throat. "How are things? I forgot to ask you about your birthing initiative last I saw you."

Laurel's face lightens almost imperceptibly at the mention of whatever it is Raiden is talking about.

"Wonderful," she says, and Turin squeezes her hand. "We had a successful delivery two days ago. A little boy."

Babies.

I frown.

The queen is ... helping women give birth? Fae women, probably. There are often complications in fae births. High fatalities for both mother and child, and that's after they've been lucky enough to conceive. Or so I've heard.

But a *queen* helping?

Raiden smiles gently, *lovingly*, as a son would.

"Will you stay for dinner?" Turin asks, his voice mesmerising. I find myself studying him, the way his eyes linger on his wife, never leaving her for long. One hand still holds Laurel's, large but gentle, his other hand resting on her shoulder. His voice.

His *voice.*

If Raiden responds, I don't hear it, too wrapped up in Turin.

In this feeling that awakens in my chest and the headache that pounds behind my eyes.

Laurel looks up at him, her mouth moving but I don't focus on the words, only that face. The softness. I can almost picture how radiant a smile would look on her.

Turin speaks again, that voice moving through my body.

I snatch the glasses from my face, rubbing my forehead, trying to ease the ache in my head as Turin continues speaking. As Laurel's soft tones join his.

I palm my eyes, rubbing so hard I see spots.

"Zara."

That one word pierces my thoughts, my pain. One word adrift in a sea of other, meaningless words.

And something inside me snaps in two.

Raiden

"I CAN'T STAY," I say, resisting the urge to look into the other room. To look for *her*. "I have a meeting out of town."

"Anything we should know?" Turin asks, glancing at Laurel.

They're having a bad day. I knew it the moment I saw them. And I have the one thing that could make this sorrow end. But it's too early. Zara isn't ready. And that could make things worse. So, I keep my news to myself even though it hurts, and shake my head.

"Just confirming a report."

"About the assassin?" Laurel asks.

The question catches me off guard, but they knew I was searching for Kyler Thames.

"Yes." I'm not really lying to them. I'm *not*.

"One more thing then," Turin says, puzzlement entering his voice. "You bought a pencil?"

"An expensive pencil," Laurel adds. "Not that we can't afford it ..."

"Oh." I look between them, my lips parted, stomach dropping.

I can't tell them

I can't tell them yet and that man has gone and ruined it.

"Raiden?" Laurel asks, concern etching her brow at my silence.

"I know it's odd." I clear my throat. "But the timing isn't right. Please, can you wait another week?"

Their frowns deepen, but they slowly nod.

"I can't see what you need it for, but we trust you," Laurel says, her eyes still searching mine.

"Thank you." I hesitate. "I have to go if I'm to make this meeting."

"Of course," Laurel says. "We'll hear from you again soon?"

"You will," I promise.

I circle back to the ballroom after parting ways with the king and queen, my thoughts still on them. I could have told them. I should have. I should have just explained everything. But Zara is a wildcard. It would be better to wait until she's remembered, until she's not quite so ... fiery.

Yes.

I shove the guilt away.

This is right.

"Eilah?" I murmur, finally striding across the room towards that pillar. "Time to go."

Silence.

My heart jumps.

"Eilah?"

I break into a jog. She can see me from there. She knows I'm here. So why isn't she coming out?

"Eilah?"

I round the pillar.

No. No. No!

She promised.

She *promised*.

But she's gone.

25

Zara

IT'S TRUE. OH, IT'S *true.*

I remember that room now. The cot and the sead-ragons flying overhead. The waterbuck and the swan. My mother's smile, my father's voice.

Mother—Hera, she lied. More than that, somehow she had my own memories hidden from me. What few I had were gone, blocked. But now they're back, and all there is now is emptiness.

Emptiness that slowly gives way to rage. An icy heart, she always says. Well now it's burning.

I abandon my hiding place before Raiden and my parents have finished talking, slipping from the room as the ghost that I am.

The guards walking the halls don't notice me as I waft from hiding place to hiding place, my body moving while my mind is frozen, whirling. I walk down the front step, slip into the stables—noticeable by its overwhelming scent of hay and horse. The stable boy is in the back room, his master nowhere to be seen. I slide a bridle from the rack and tack up the first horse I see.

Then I simply walk out, leading the horse beside me.

Thievery is all about confidence. That's one of my rules, but I can't remember which one. Doesn't seem so important anymore.

Raiden still has my bag, though he didn't have it with him in the ballroom. So I nick another one as I pass through the town. I slip a cloak from a stall and tuck it inside my overalls, the bulge making me appear months past due date but the stall owner is too busy to notice my sloppy work, anyway.

Two loafs of bread, a waterskin, and a pocketful of freshly picked kilan berries later and I'm mounting up and leaving the city far behind.

I turn the horse southeast, lean into the saddle, and push the gelding into a gallop. Towards the desert.

Towards home.

Towards my prison.

Towards Mother.

The road is silent without my shadow. It's refreshing.

And lonely.

But it means that my mind has nowhere to go but backwards. Back to the few, little memories that have resurfaced. More snapshots than any real substance. But *there*. My head no longer pounds, stopping that moment the memories came back. But a deep ache inside of me has taken its place. I let the rage swallow it. I let it swallow everything until there is nothing left.

Days pass in a steady routine of travel, sleep, and more travel. I push the horse as far as it can go without hurting it. I steal what I need. And with every day, the desert draws closer. And I still don't know what I will say. What I will *do*. All I know, is I want answers. And I want blood.

The nights begin to warm as I pass over the border of Frigarth and enter the nomadic lands between the city of water and the endless sand. I recoil at the familiarity of it even as my body relaxes.

The fire flickering over my small campsite is hardly needed, but the crackle and popping of wood is comforting in my solitude. It mixes with the song of crickets and nightbirds as I stare at the stars.

"What the hell are you doing?" Elvar yells, his large form appearing over me in a rustle of feathers. About time. He caught up with me three hours ago.

"Debating the pros and cons of gutting someone. It's a little messy, but it's just so *worth* it."

I can't see his face, framed in fire and cast in shadow, but I imagine it pales as he shifts his feet.

"Where are you going?"

I sigh, sitting up, that fire bubbling beneath the surface. "I'm in no mood for this, Elvar."

"You're not in the mood?" His tone is tight, his fists clenched. He's been mulling over this for a while.

"Yes," I snap.

"Too bad! I've been searching for you for a week! Do you know how worried I was when I went to fetch you and you were gone?"

I grin, more of a baring of my teeth than an actual smile. "Did you think I'd gone to kill them?"

He drops to a crouch in front of me, throwing his face into the light. His anger has made his face hard. My own rises in challenge to his.

"I didn't know what to think. I had the whole palace searched and had to lie through my teeth to the king and queen."

"How dreadful."

His eyes narrow. "What. Are. You. Doing?"

I lean forwards, so there are only inches between our faces. "None. Of. Your. Business!" I spit, rocking back and jumping to my feet.

"I suggest you move on, Elvar," I say, putting space between us. "We're done. I held up to my end of the deal. I went to your palace. I saw your beloved royals. And now I'm done."

"Why?" He straightens, following. "What about your mission?"

He says the word bitterly, but I can see the confusion in his eyes. This is not the reaction he expected at all.

"I wasn't supposed to be there in the first place. I need to speak with Mother before I do anything."

"You're going back?" The hollow words fall off his tongue, his body deflating.

"I'm going home." The word is sour in my mouth, but true. It's the only home I've ever known.

"Home?" he growls, latching onto the anger instead of disappointment. Oh, we are so alike. "Then you're heading in the wrong direction!"

"I don't think I am, Elvar. But I do think it's time for you to leave."

He clenches his jaw, plants his feet. "No."

Wrong move.

"No?" I stalk towards him, my breath frost on the air.

"I'm not leaving you again."

"Oh, I can tell you that you will," I growl, my canines beginning to form, lengthen, "but whether you're still alive or not will be up to you."

His eyes linger on the leopard's teeth. He gulps, but the idiot doesn't stop. Doesn't back down.

"Why are you doing this?"

When the claws break through my skin, I stamp down on the magic, reminding it who's in charge. But the sight sends Elvar's eyes wide. Satisfaction drips to my core.

"Because I remember everything," I murmur, "and someone has to pay."

I smile, my canines cutting my lips and blood trickles down my chin. "And why not you?"

I leap at him.

26

Raiden

Z ARA LUNGES, THE SNOW leopard roaring at me from behind her eyes. Rage has consumed her. And I'm the only thing around. The only person she can unleash on.

So be it.

Her hands remain empty, her steel daggers still at her sides, and her ice magic forgotten or unwanted. So, I leave my own weapons sheathed and block her every blow. Her shoulder no longer holding her back.

Her fist jabs at my face, and I've barely dodged before she follows with a steady combination of kicks.

She's flawless, even in her rage. Each move a dance she's known her whole life, her lean body moving effortlessly.

I do nothing but block and dodge, not even attempting to throw a punch. And even though she lands many blows, my inaction makes her angrier.

"Punch me!" she screams, claws coming for my face.

"Zara," I pant, ducking and stepping away.

She roars, closing the distance with a jumping kick that lands heavily on my shoulder.

Grunting, I step closer, inside her kicking range. Her eyes gleam.

"Eilah."

But my voice triggers another series of attacks that leave me battered and bruised despite my attempts to dodge. Blood trickles from a cut to my forehead, my ribs ache, and my shoulder throbs.

I have years of training behind me, and I don't stand a chance.

"Eilah," I pant, grabbing her shoulders. "Stop."

"Why?" she growls, throwing me off. "So you can take me back to the palace?"

"No, let me—"

It happens in the blink of an eye. Zara drops to the ground, her leg sweeping out in a seamless motion and then I am gasping for air on my back.

She crouches over me, her arms and legs holding me down, her hair hanging down in a thick curtain. I don't move, don't wriggle beneath her, and don't throw her off.

"This is nice," I gasp, my lungs still trying to draw air back in.

Her hands grow colder, not painful, but uncomfortable.

"Eilah," I say, breaths coming easier now. "Let me help you."

Her eyes narrow. "Help me?"

"Your battles are my battles," I repeat. Insist.

Her head tilts, every bit the predator even in her fae form.

"You want justice," she says, echoing my words from the Conquered Lands.

"I want justice."

Her grip loosens, but she doesn't move. Her eyes hold mine, stormy and filled with fire.

"If you make a move against me, Raiden Elvar, I will not hesitate to end you. I don't care if you have good intentions, if you think you're helping me. I will kill you."

This time, I believe her.

I nod, and she slowly removes herself from on top of me and retreats back to her measly bed of a cloak and blanket.

I stay there a moment longer, aware of her eyes still on me. She may be a woman, but right now, she is more leopard than fae, and I keep my movements slow, unthreatening.

Zara is silent in the early light of dawn, but I decide to pretend nothing happened. If I found out my entire life was a lie, I imagine I would go feral, too. I *am* angry, not at her, but for her and I've only known her for a couple months.

She still wants to go back to the assassins, wherever it is they live. She's never revealed where she's from, but something tells me she will now.

"Where are we going?"

Zara chews her lip, staring into the coals of last night's fire.

"The Kilduin," she says.

My brows rise, but taking in her tanned form, it makes sense. Where better to hide and train a compound full of assassins than the desert?

I stand, wincing as I do. Her eyes snap to me, remorse in those stormy eyes, but she says nothing. Luckily my ribs are merely bruised, and my shoulder doesn't seem to have sustained any lasting damage. Even if it is sore. But I still can't find it within myself to be angry at her. She's trying to deal with this in the sole way she knows how. She needs someone to help her.

"Do you have a plan?" I probe, unsure if she means to return home or destroy it. Honestly, I think she could go either way right now. The way I'm feeling, I could definitely help with that last option.

"I'm working on one."

"Will you tell me?"

"Maybe." She stands, turning to saddle the horse she stole from the palace. The horse master would have fired that stableboy if I hadn't stepped in.

I stare at her back, realisation hitting me as my shoulder throbs again. "I won't be able to fly."

"That sounds like a *you* problem."

"Hmm," I say, crossing to her side. "And yet, it doesn't."

"Fine," she growls, "you can ride behind me. But tomorrow you're back to flying."

I smirk, trying to coax her free of her anger. "Don't enjoy the idea of being close to me?"

Zara instantly rises to my challenge, her demeanour changing as she turns to face me. Her eyes linger on my lips as she leans forwards, so close I can feel her icy breath.

"Exactly," she purrs.

I chuckle.

"And the two of us on the horse will only slow us down."

"Keep telling yourself that," I murmur, brushing my nose with hers.

She pulls back with a huff, yet I can almost see a smile trying to break through.

"Let's go. I'll cut those hands off if I feel them on my hips."

"I'm sure you will."

"What did you mean by again?" Zara says abruptly, her voice bouncing in time with the horse.

"What?" I frown. Despite her warning, my hands have remained attached to my arms, even though they rest on her hips. To help me keep balance.

"You said you'd never leave me again. What's again?"

"Oh." I rub my chin. It's not something I enjoy talking about, but for her ... "I couldn't save you. That night."

Zara's silent for a long moment and I can almost hear her mind working.

"Were you my guard?"

"No."

"Then—"

"I was too late!" I cut her off, then wince apologetically. "You were already gone when I got there."

"I wasn't your responsibility, and you were bleeding out. I saw the blood, remember?"

I don't respond, because none of that matters. I should have been there. I should have stopped them. As a palace guard, it was my duty.

"Did you mean it?" she asks, yanking me from the memories.

"Hmm?"

"That you won't leave me," Zara says quietly.

I pause, wanting her to understand the truth in my words. "I meant it."

"Because you want to atone," she says thoughtfully. But the words don't sit right.

"No. I don't think so."

"Because I'm your princess then."

"Yes." *And no.* Even if she wasn't ... parting would hurt. I know she is angry, full of revenge, confused, with no idea of who she is. And yet, I find myself drawn to her. The thought of not being near her hurts. Despite it all. Despite the shoulder that throbs, the ribs that protest each bounce of the horse. The scar I'll carry for the rest of my life. Parting would hurt more. So I purse my lips and admit, "and no."

She stiffens against my form, but soon relaxes. I consider it a step forwards from the death threat she once would have promised.

"I see."

A woman of many words.

"Don't worry, you can still hate me."

"Oh, I do."

I laugh. "Glad that's sorted."

And yet, I don't think she does. Not really, not truly.

I think she hates everything. And maybe she hates me a little less.

27

Zara

E LVAR SOMEHOW MANAGES TO spend another day on
the back of my horse, and I tell myself I don't enjoy it. I pretend my mind doesn't linger on his hands at
my hips. I keep my voice uncaring even as I hang on his
every word, dreading the long silences where I'm left to
my thoughts. The struggle continues across campfire after
campfire, growing worse as he spends the days in the air
again.

Somehow, Elvar has become a light in the darkness that
swirls around me.

A flame of a different kind that both consumes me and
keeps the cold at bay.

I hate it.

But not as much as I should.

Despite his closeness, I can't bring myself to ask about my parents, my old life. It would feel too real. As if acknowledging it any further would change everything, including me.

"Tell me about Hera."

My head snaps up at his voice, drowsiness gone. Elvar sits beside me on the flattened grass, staring into the fire as if he never spoke. And for a moment I let myself pretend he didn't, even if my mind clings to the sound of his voice.

"She's an assassin," the words finally come.

"Obviously."

I roll my eyes, but his are now fixed on me.

"Tell me," he murmurs.

"She's my mother," I say, even if it's not true now. "She's a hard woman. She's always pushed me to be the best. But she's kept me alive. Kept me healthy. Strong."

Elvar nods, thoughtfully. "Alive, but not living."

"I suppose."

"Did she really think you would kill Aeris?" he says, twisting to face me fully now. Leaves crunch under him.

"Yes," I say, refusing to turn to him. She did, and she had no reason to think I wouldn't.

"Have you done it before? Killed a brother or sister?"

I frown, glancing at him. His eyes are open, honest, no judgement to be seen. He wants to understand. Not at all like Sorren. And somehow, he can coax things out of me I have never voiced before.

"Once," I finally say, forcing my voice to remain light. Uncaring. "But he was new, and he tried to escape. So Mother added him to our poisons class."

He shifts. "You tested poisons on him?"

"On many people," I say. "Some of them were targets, some were merely unlucky enough to be travelling through the Kilduin. Mother found uses for them all. We fought them, tortured them, healed them. Whatever we needed to learn, they were there to practice on."

"Did you ever practice on each other?"

Elvar's hand finds my knee, gentle and tender despite the calluses. I stare at it, but I can't bring myself to shove him away. There's something cathartic in answering him.

"Yes. But we have healers. It was never permanent," I say, glancing at him. Mother was very particular about what wounds were healed and what weren't.

"That doesn't make it better." Firelight flickers over his face, highlighting the sharp corners. His eyes. His mouth.

"No, it doesn't," I admit quietly.

"It needs to stop."

"It's normal," I say, trying to lighten my voice. Trying not to acknowledge what I've always known.

"No, it isn't."

That Mother is a monster.

That I am one too.

"No. It isn't."

"Eilah, you're next."

197

I lift my chin, meeting Mother's hard, green eyes. Her voice rings out over us, even as the last student is carried away, his blood soaking into the sand.

It's Cutting Day.

Mother's eyes narrow. I can't make her call me again. It'll only make it worse. I force my rebellious legs to work, to drag themselves through the sand, leaving the false safety of the shadow of the tower behind. I stop in front of her, turning to face the remaining brothers and sisters waiting their turn. Aeris's face is pale under her shock of red hair, but her eyes are hard, her back straight.

Good.

We can't afford to be weak.

I wipe my sweaty palms and pull a dagger from its sheath.

The healers reappear, swiftly crossing to stand beside me, their hands hovering millimeters from my skin in preparation.

Sweat courses down my back, sticking my shirt to my skin. I'm grateful it's such a hot day, because it's not the temperature causing my discomfit.

I raise the knife.

"Ready?" Mother says, her callused hand closing around mine.

I lick my lips. Clear my throat.

"Ready."

And my blood soaks deep into the sand.

"Zara! Zara!"

Rough hands shake me and before I'm fully awake, I've rolled the person, my body holding theirs down, glinting dagger at their throat. The first streaks of dawn are on the horizon and a trail of smoke rises from the coals of the fire.

"Zara," Raiden gasps, hands open in surrender. "It's OK. It's OK."

Sweat drips from my nose, coats my face and back. My breath comes ragged.

A dream. It was a dream.

Elvar's words echo my thoughts. "It was just a dream. It's not real."

I stare at the knife at his throat, the same one that cut my own.

"But it was," I murmur, ignoring the way my eyes blur.

He reaches for my face, but I drop the blade, stumbling away from him, running a hand through my knotted hair.

Elvar's beside me in an instant. "What was?"

I close my eyes, fingers rising to trace the thin scar at my throat. My scarf is gone. I must have torn it off in my sleep. It's been a long time since I've dreamed of the Cutting. It was exactly as I remember it.

I shudder.

A rough hand grips mine, but it's gentle, completely unlike Mother's.

"Tell me about it," he coaxes.

I shake my head, and all it does is release the tears I'd been holding back.

"Zara." His fingers brush them away. "Was she the one holding the knife?"

My eyes fly open. Elvar's eyes are glued to me, studying me. *Seeing* me.

Mother.

I suppose we talked about her. It makes sense I'd dream of her.

I guess his thoughts have gone the same way.

I gulp. "In a way."

"What do you mean?" His hands linger on my cheeks.

"It was my hand holding the knife. And her hand holding mine," I whisper.

His eyes widen, and anger flares. "She made you—she made you cut your own throat?"

I nod, refusing to let another tear fall even as they form.

"I was twelve," I admit, sniffing.

"Zara." He pauses. "I'm going to try something. And I would greatly appreciate it if you didn't stab me."

"Um, OK."

His arms encircle me.

And it's kind of nice.

I'm not sure I've ever been hugged like this, and I find myself melting into his warmth.

His cheek rests against my head, his arms holding me close. My arms seem to rise of their own accord, and wrap themselves around his strong form, my fists clinging to his shirt.

I fit just right. Like I was made to be there.

We stay that way until my eyes dry, until my heart settles, and my mind slowly returns to itself, and my new rule rises to the forefront of my thoughts.

I reluctantly lower my arms and clear my throat. "OK, drawing really close to stabbing time."

"Oh." He releases me with a chuckle. "Right."

I hurry back to my blanket and cloak, throwing myself down on the hard ground. Wrapping my body as tightly as I can in the cloak, I ignore the way I wish he could still comfort me.

"Go back to sleep," I grunt. There's no way I'm going back to sleep with dawn on the horizon, but that doesn't matter.

"Goodnight, Zara," he murmurs, moving silently back to his place.

"Goodnight, shadow."

By the time the sun has fully risen over the horizon, a plan has formed entirely in my mind, but I keep it to myself. There is much to be done, and I want to be prepared before we arrived at the compound. Besides, it'll keep my mind off the nightmare and what followed.

I almost don't notice when the hard earth below us turns into compact sand, except that my mind reminds me we'll need water.

There's water in the desert if you know where to find it, but I also don't want to start our journey with a low supply. So, I wheel the horse towards the last settlement before the Kilduin, my rook following easily in the sky.

I have two waterskins, thanks to Elvar remembering to bring my backpack along with him. I pull them out at the village well, ignoring the way the locals' gazes linger on me. For many, their eyes are the one part of them visible beneath their protection against the sun.

The rook lands on the bucket, sending water spraying as it rocks.

I glare at him. "I'm using that."

He caws, dipping his beak in to scoop water into his mouth.

Thirsty.

"Fine," I say, unscrewing the lid of the second bottle. "Drink your fill, but be quick. Desert people don't trust strangers."

Not with all the stories that float around, many of them encouraged by Mother.

"Can we help you, miss?" a rough voice says from behind me. The man's been staring from under the eaves of a ragged house for so long I was beginning to wonder if he could move that large frame of his.

"Nope," I say lightly, not bothering to glance his way. I already know everything worth knowing about him. His arms are nearly as large as my head, his thighs even bigger. Tattoos decorate his body, some in images of beasts, some in swirls. And his eyes are hard, distrusting, and fixed on me.

He's a large man, but those muscles will get in the way.

Probably not the best person to elect as warden but here we are.

The rook, pauses, catching my eye.

I subtly shake my head, the corner of my mouth rising. I'd hardly need help if this man decided to cause trouble. In fact, I'd welcome a chance to unleash a little.

"Will you be staying long?" the man grunts, closer now.

I tuck a strand of hair behind my ear. "As long as I need to prepare for my journey."

"And the rook?"

I shrug. "Seems the bird's thirsty."

Said rook shoots me a glare in warning and hops off the bucket.

Sighing, I tip the remaining water into the empty bottle.

"Say," I spin, facing the man, "you don't know anyone in need of a horse? I find I have no need for mine."

His eyes narrow. "Headed into the Kilduin?"

"Yep," I let the word pop.

"You'd be best going around," he says flatly.

"Oh, but I so want to go through."

The warden's eyes sweep over me, lingering on my daggers. His hand twitches.

"On your own head," he finally mutters. "Gilan will take it." He jerks his head at a small building down the street.

"Great, if you'll step out of my way, I can head over there. Then I'll be gone even quicker."

I can practically feel Elvar's little rook eyes boring into the back of my head, but honestly, the man *is* in the way.

The large man grins, though it doesn't meet his eyes. I match the smile with my own.

Come on.

He huffs and turns away, deeming me unworthy of his wrath, I suppose. Ha!

Elvar pecks my hand right as I open my mouth to call after him.

"Ow!" I frown. "I was just going to thank him."

He fixes me with another glare, and I bite my lip to hide the genuine smile that threatens to break out. Glares are a strange expression on a rook.

"Come on," I say, grabbing the reins of the horse. "We need to get moving."

I follow the man's directions to Gilan's home, refusing to acknowledge what a shame it is to leave this horse behind. It's a beauty, but horses don't belong in the desert.

I don't feel any guilt for taking it from—from those people. Consider it a birthday gift. They've missed a few, after all. So, there's no guilt for selling it either.

A flutter of large wings sounds behind me, and without turning, I know the rook has landed on the horse. I shake my head at the image, while reaching out to knock on Gilan's door.

Fae and human homes alike are enclosed this close to the desert. The scorching sun and high winds kicking up sand make it a necessity. Though I've never seen many fae here—most can't stand it.

"What?" The door flies open and a middle-aged human man stands before me, long hair braided away from a face covered in so much hair he wouldn't need a headscarf.

I raise my eyebrows.

"I'm told you want a horse."

The man glances at the gelding, taking its measure in a single moment.

"Perhaps." He's impressed and trying to hide it.

"Either you do, or you don't. The beast is three hundred coins."

His eyes widen. "Three hundred?"

"Yep," I say. "Came from the palace stables in Frigarth. Be a good breeder."

"It's a gelding."

I shrug. "Would have been a good breeder."

Gilan's eyes narrow, and after a long moment he throws back his head and laughs loud and long.

Elvar caws behind me.

"I like you!" Gilan says around a wheeze, laughter trying to break through again. "I'll give you two hundred."

"Deal," I say, grinning.

28

Zara

"**Y**OU DON'T HAVE TO walk with me."

"I know," Elvar says, two steps behind me, feet slipping in the loose sand.

I wipe my forehead, glancing at the hot sun. It's still early, not even midmorning yet, and I'm drenched in sweat. Nothing like going home,

I stop, dropping my bag in front of me to dig inside.

"Here." I throw a strip of fabric at Elvar. "Wrap your head and face. You'll need it."

He holds it awkwardly in front of him. "Er ..."

I roll my eyes, hiding a smile. "They only had purple, Elvar. Man up."

They didn't.

He shakes his head. "No, how do I put it on?"

"You want me to dress you?"

"Zara," he says, shoulders dropping.

I bite back the apology before it can escape, reminding myself of my new rule.

"Fine, give it here." I grab it from his hands, and set to wrapping, protecting him from the sun. "You'll have to learn how to do this. We're still days out."

"OK," he says, a little unsure. Who would have thought *this* is what would ruffle him?

"You've never been out here before, have you?"

"No," he says, reaching up to touch the fabric, but I slap his hand away. I guess that makes sense. A man from the nation of water wouldn't know what to do in a desert. Most fae don't.

"Well," I say, stepping back to admire my handiwork. "Do what I say, and you might live."

"Or you might kill me," he says, voice muffled under the headscarf, "you've only threatened my life a dozen times."

I shrug. "Guess you won't know."

"What about you?" he asks, fiddling with the strip across his mouth and nose.

I free my scarf from around my neck, and with quick movements, copy the covering on Elvar, leaving a small strip of skin across my eyes open to the hot air.

"Put these on too," I say, throwing him a pair of boots, bought with the money from Gilan. "Your feet will burn."

"I hate shoes," he murmurs, awkwardly pulling them onto his feet. My own are already covered.

"Just hope we don't run into a sandstorm."

Elvar's eyes widen, looking up with one shoe on.

"And I hadn't even thought about the Morsang," I add.

Instead of widening further, his eyes narrow. "That's a myth."

"Oh?" I sling my bag back over my shoulder and set off again. "Is it? I suppose you don't believe dragons exist?"

"No," Elvar says, the jolt in his voice telling me he's slipped in the sand again.

"Then how come my aunt could turn into one?" I turn to face him, walking backwards. "There's a reason she was called the Dragon Assassin. Fae shapeshifters can't make up a form. It has to be real."

He gapes at me.

"Better stay close, shadow."

We rest in the sparse shadow of a sand dune through the hottest hours of the day, waiting until dusk to continue on again. The desert is always bright at night, with nothing to block the glow of the stars and moon from hitting the ground. To fae eyes, it's almost as light as day. I keep strict control of our water, diverting to top up our waterskins from even the smallest source.

"Here," I say, grunting as I pull a clump of long grass from a dune. "Suck on the ends of this."

Elvar frowns, waiting for a trick. "You first."

Rolling my eyes, I split the clump in two, tear off the roots, pull my scarf down and suck on the end. Bitter liquid instantly fills my mouth.

He takes his half from my still outstretched hand.

"Every drop is lifesaving out here, Elvar."

He nods, chewing on the stems, squinting against the strong sunlight.

"We'll stop here for a moment," I say. Because there's something else here that I want.

"Wait here," I say, setting off for the nearest sand dune.

"Where are you going?"

I huff, pulling my scarf back up. "To relieve myself, soldier. Would you like to come?"

His mouth forms a thin line. "No."

"Good."

It takes me ten minutes to get over the hill, two minutes to pick what I need and shove it inside my bag, and only five to return since I slide my way down the dune. Elvar is sitting where I left him, and I can't help but laugh at the lost expression on his face. The desert has turned my warrior shadow into a nervous child.

He scowls. "What?"

"Nothing," I say, patting his shoulder as I walk past. "Let's go. We can get another hour in before it's too hot."

Something rustles behind me.

Sand.

Lots and lots of sand sliding downwards.

My heart drops.

"Elvar," I say, calmly pulling out my daggers as I turn. "Get out your swords."

He doesn't question, doesn't hesitate, but pulls both swords from their scabbards and spins, his gaze following mine.

The dune I slid down moments ago rises, sand pouring down its sides in an avalanche.

"Morsang?"

"No." I step closer, peering through the orange cascade. My eyes widen as they snag on a flash of dark red armour.

"Scorpus."

"What?" Elvar yells, shuffling backwards to my side.

It would be better to run, but there's not exactly anywhere to hide out here.

"Its armour is weakest at the joints," I say, quickly. "Stay clear of the tail."

Elvar nods, swinging a sword loosely in his grip.

And that's when the sand dune explodes.

And out of it flies a scorpion twenty feet tall, the dripping barb on its tail nearly as long as me.

"Big one," I grunt. "Left!"

I dive into Elvar as the scorpus's plated back arches upwards and the barb shoots forwards. We roll across the sand, coming to a stop with my body strewn across his. I'm up before I can linger, yelling at him to move.

"We need to get in close!"

"That should be easy!" he shouts, ducking as a pincer flies over his head. It could cut him in two with ease.

"Shut up, Elvar!" I yell, sprinting forwards, zig zagging to keep the scorpus distracted.

"What happens if we get the venom on us?"

"Don't!"

"Oh, that's helpful!" he grunts, dodging another attack.

The scorpus is focused on him, both pincers lashing out, leaving me forgotten.

Guess my shadow is good for something after all.

I dive under it, the sun completely blocked out by its bulk.

The underside of the scorpus is lighter, more orange than the red of its back armour. And its softer. But my daggers won't pierce it. I need to find a weak point. A search that definitely isn't working with how much the beast is moving.

"Will you stop making it move?" I shout, as the animal lurches.

Elvar doesn't bother to reply, rolling aside as the barb shoots for him again.

"Always the hard way," I mutter, titling my head back. I try to match my movements with the beasts, scurrying backwards and forwards as I try to pinpoint the weakest point with the best vital organs. Somewhere in its chest would be best.

"There!" I shout, plunging my dagger upwards.

The scorpus screeches and before I can tear the dagger along the seam I've found, the body lowers.

"Oh no."

I dive aside, taking my dagger with me, right as the beast slams into the ground, then turns its angry eyes on me. A thorn is in its chest. And I put it there.

"What did you do?" Elvar yells, taking advantage of the scorpus's distraction and aiming a swing at a joint in its leg.

His sword comes down with a clang and the beast screeches again, its leg jolting, slamming into him. He goes flying.

The large scorpion rises from the ground, but I doubt I'll be able to sneak back under it. I sheath my blades. What I really need is a spear, or a halberd. Something with a very long blade, or very long reach. But my ice will melt quickly out here, using more magic to form and stay intact. Which means I need to make this count.

Elvar is back on his feet, tearing his crooked headscarf from his face.

"I need to get in front of its face."

"That's a terrible idea!" he pants, sand clinging to his clothes.

"It's the only one I have."

Shaking his head, he dashes forwards. "I'll keep it busy."

"Thought you would."

I run, the sand grabbing at my ankles as I pump my legs harder.

Elvar darts in and out, aiming slashes and strikes at any joint he can find. It keeps those pincers busy enough to allow me to duck inside their range and into the space where the beast can't see me. Its eyes are on the top and sides of its head. Meaning that the place directly in front of his huge mandibles is completely blind. I'm not sure if that's a good thing or not.

I only have a moment before it moves. I throw back my arm, draw the magic up, as much as I can muster as quickly as I can, and send an ice spear nearly as long as my own body straight through the little gap between its mandibles.

No sound leaves the scorpus this time as it stumbles backwards, the ground shaking beneath me.

"Zara! Look out!"

Something hard slams into me, and my arm burns as I go flying. My body slams into the ground and I gain a face full of sand.

"Zara!"

I splutter, shoving my arms under me, my headscarf skewed, hair loose and sand covering every inch of me.

I spit a glob of it from my mouth.

"Are you OK?" Elvar asks, skidding to a stop beside me.

"Fine," I grunt, glancing over my shoulder to find the scorpus unmoving.

I press a hand to my head. It took more magic than I'll ever admit to keep that spear from melting, and the ache in my head proves it.

"Your arm," Elvar says, tenderly reaching for me.

"What?"

A trail of blood stains my sleeve, starting near my shoulder and already reaching my elbow.

I sigh. "That explains the pain."

Elvar grins, shaking his head. "You are one crazy woman."

I shrug, wincing at the movement.

"Let's get you fixed up."

Raiden

The moon is bright tonight. Thousands of stars shining around it, not a cloud in the sky. I sigh, turning back towards camp, where Zara waits for me. I can't see her from here, but she's probably asleep by now. She used a lot of energy fighting that beast, not that she'd admit it.

I shake my head. That scorpus nearly killed us both. Twice. And if Zara is right, it isn't our only problem out here.

I set off back to camp, bladder a little lighter, but mind and body still equally as heavy. I'm glad that caravan was passing through, though. A camel will make this trip go faster.

Zara is sitting up, her hands inside her bag when I return. "Are you all right?"

"Yes," she says, closing the bag.

The camel grunts from where we've left it, front leg hobbled so it can't leave us.

Though the night would be dark to a human, it is merely dim to us. It's a good thing, since a fire would be impossible to start out here with no fuel.

"Just checking our water supply," she murmurs.

Zara hesitates. "Thank you," she says, voice soft. "For helping me today."

My eyebrows rise. "Are you sure you're feeling OK?"

She chuckles. "Don't push it, Elvar."

I sit on my blanket, sprawled on the sand some three meters away from her, but she pushes to her feet and shuffles over to me.

"Can I talk to you for a minute?" She wraps her arms around herself. Unsure. I've never seen her unsure.

"What is it?"

She sits heavily beside me, refusing to look at me. I find my focus zeroing in on her.

"Do you think—" She purses her lips. "—Do you think my parents will forgive me?"

Her words are a pang in my chest. "There's nothing to forgive, Zara."

She frowns. "I've killed a lot of people, Raiden."

I pretend the sound of my name on her lips isn't music to my ears.

"You were raised to be a killer."

"That doesn't excuse it."

Zara still won't look at me, and by instinct, I reach out and turn her face towards me.

"You didn't know the truth of who you are." My thumb brushes her jaw.

"And you do?" she whispers. I can see the ghost of a memory in her eyes, the whisper of a name on her lips.

"I'm not Sorren, Zara. I already know who you are."

A tinge of red flushes her cheeks, matching the pink of her lips.

"I'm sorry," I say, hand moving away from her face. "This was about your parents."

"It can be about us."

Us.

The word lingers in the air between us, even as her eyes slowly fall to my lips.

"I meant it," I murmur, needing her to believe me. "I won't leave you."

Her lips twitch, a smile lurking just out of reach. I would do anything to set it free.

"Zara ..."

She answers my question, my yearning with a nod, leaning forwards. She's been this close before, so many times, when she teases, matches my games, but this time there is no light to her eyes. No glint.

Her lips press against mine, soft and sweet and hesitant. My hand tangles in her long hair cascading down her back, her own sliding to my face as her lips meet mine again.

"I'm sorry, Raiden," she murmurs against my lips.

"What for?"

She pulls back, shaking her head, but she's blurry, her form blending into the endless sand behind her.

No.

The word doesn't make it past my lips. My lips still with the sweet tang of hers on them.

The world goes black.

29

Zara

THE TOWER APPEARS TWO days later, its apex glinting in the light, the sun shining off the grey stone.
One of my siblings will be up there keeping an eye out for
trespassers. An apt punishment for whatever error they've
made. The hot sun reflects up into their faces from the
stone of the tower, increasing the temperature by up to five
degrees. More than one trainee has had to spend the night
in the infirmary after a post up there.

I grin at the sight, raise an arm and wave.

A horn rings out across the dunes, echoing over the compound and its training grounds. It rings once more, long
and wavering.

The call of welcome.

The call of home.

I drag the camel into a faster walk behind me, Elvar's bound body swaying in time with its movements. I've had to give him another dose from that little flower I collected in the dunes twice now, and this latest should wear off soon.

Just in time to meet Mother.

"Eilah. We were beginning to worry."

"No, you weren't, Darius," I say, meeting his dark stare. Darius stands in the arch of the gateway to the compound, arms crossed over his leather armour. A utilitarian suit similar to my own is under it, lined with pockets and keeping much of his skin covered from the hot desert sun.

I hold his glare.

A grin breaks out across my brother's face and he dives forwards, surprising me with a hug. "Where have you been?"

"Jobs took longer than expected," I say, extracting myself from his long arms. Darius has always been tall, long and lanky, but it's deceiving. He's as strong and skilled as the rest of us. I jerk my head at Elvar, whose eyes flutter as he tries to throw off the drug. "And I had a shadow that wouldn't go away."

Darius's eyes hardly land on him before they're back on me. "You didn't try very hard if he's here."

"He's from Frigarth." I cross my arms. "And close to the king and queen."

Darius's gaze returns to Elvar, this time with interest. My shadow can't hold his eyes open yet, but I have no doubt he can hear every word spoken.

"Mother would like to meet him," my brother says.

"Exactly."

"Come, Nina's gone to get Mother." Darius gestures for me to follow him through the open gate.

"Nina?" I swallow, giving the camel's lead a yank. "How is she?"

He grins over his shoulder. "You know Nina, she just wants to get out there."

"I do." I think back to our conversation in the forest outside Southlily, how excited she was at the prospect of a job.

"Does she have a job?" I ask, shooting Darius a knowing smile as we pass through the small tunnel separating the gate from the rest of the compound.

"Nope," he laughs, "but that won't stop her. She's gotten good, you know?"

"It's not up to her."

"No," he says.

All thoughts of conversation flee from my mind as we exit the tunnel and the compound opens up before me. It's been so long since I was home.

My brothers and sisters fill the first training yard, locked in combat in twos, threes, and some in large groups. Some fight with their fists, some with knives, lances, axes, and magic. All the girls have hair long enough to rival mine, while all the boys wear theirs shaved so fine it's hard to tell they even have hair. Mother says it's to push us harder, to make us even stronger. If we can beat our brothers even with such long hair tripping us up, then we can fight anyone.

Three healers in white robes walk the border of the yard, their eyes flying from combat to combat. They're not to be underestimated though, Mother trained them as hard as the rest of us.

"I'll see you later," Darius says, drawing my attention back, "I'm supposed to train the newbies in five minutes."

"Oh, joy."

He grins. "Maybe you can swing by later and scare them? They always pee themselves when they see Mother's favourite."

I slap his arm, then pause. "I'll think about it."

Rolling his eyes, Darius breaks into a jog, disappearing through one of the archways bordering the compound. He'll be headed to the second training ground, a smaller and more controlled area. For one thing, the ground isn't as compact as this one.

Everything here is sand and stone, two bland colours at war with each other for dominance. I pass through another arch, walk the wall of the dormitory for the younger girls, and turn towards the tower. Mother will be in there, ready to debrief me.

I take a deep breath. There's so much to talk about, so much to ask and explain. Starting with the shadow that is starting to grunt through his gag.

I spin on my heel, stalking towards him. "There's no use in looking for help, Elvar. Every one of my brothers and sisters will be lining up to kill you."

His blue eyes search mine, betrayal lighting them.

"Don't look at me like that," I say. "I warned you; love is for fools."

I lead the camel on without another backwards glance, pulling the scarf from my head as I go. My hair falls down my back, long and already coming loose from its braid. I'd forgotten how impossible sand makes even the basic of hair care.

"You!" I snap at a pair of boys in their mid-teens walking past. Though they have the appearance of someone who has grown too fast, their bodies are rippling with lean muscle. And covered in scars. They snap to attention. "Get that lump off my camel."

They hurry forwards while I stand back to watch. Perks of having younger siblings—though none of the people here are actually related to me or Mother.

"Watch which rope you pull!" I shout, making them jump as they reach for the one that will free too much of Elvar's movement.

"Yes, ma'am," the first boy says, slapping the second's hand away.

"What's going on here?" a voice drawls from my right.

Sighing, I turn to face my least favourite brother.

"So good to see you again, Brooks."

His silver eyes scan me head to toe from where he leans against a wall. Ever casual. "You're late, Eilah."

"Perfection takes time, dear brother."

He bares his teeth in a predator's grin and my blood rises in challenge. "Don't let being Mother's favourite get to your head. It won't always protect you."

"When has it ever?" I quip, strolling forwards. "Jobs are given based on skill, Brooks. It's not my fault if you're not up to par."

Satisfaction fills my core as his face reddens.

"Don't let that anger go to your head," I twist his words, "it won't protect you."

"You still think you're the only one getting the good jobs?" he growls.

"Oh, I know," I purr. "Because it wasn't you sent to deal with Aeris."

His fists clench and a smirk raises my lips as he realises the truth of my words. Only the most trusted would be sent to deal with a sister. And that wasn't him.

"Must go, dear brother. I don't want to be late."

Brooks doesn't move, but I sense his eyes on me as I grab the end of the rope still restraining Elvar—now with feet firmly on the ground and tied tight enough that he can barely walk—and tug him into the cool of the tower.

Mother's office is at the top. Everything is about fitness, about skill, about endurance. Anyone worthy of being sent on a mission should be able to reach the top without a problem. I can, but it's just so *annoying*. But since I have a prisoner, I can stop at the floor third from the top. Yay.

When I reach the landing, I don't bother knocking but push through the heavy door, dragging Elvar with me. He's puffing heavily through the gag, but I can't stand the thought of his talking right now. So, I leave it on.

"Ah, there you are, darling."

A tall woman stands by the chair bolted to the floor in the centre of the room. Her long red hair is loose and flows low, near her thighs. I'm told she's nearly the spitting image of Aunt Lily, even with the same freckles dotting her face.

"Mother." I smile, hurrying across the room to embrace her, breathe in that familiar scent of home. She's in her usual fighting leathers, weapons strapped to every inch of her. Even out here, we are always ready.

Nina isn't here.

Mother's face breaks into one of its rare smiles as we hug, but then she pulls away and stares pointedly at Elvar.

"And who is this? I didn't expect you to bring home a boy, Eilah," Mother tsks.

I laugh. "But I think you'll approve of this one."

Her green eyes wander up and down Elvar, lingering of the bonds.

"He's in good shape."

I resist the urge to swallow. She's not talking about his physical strength but rather the lack of damage.

"He knows much," I say. "The desert was a challenge for him, and I couldn't risk breaking him."

"Hmm." Mother turns those eyes on me, and I meet them easily. "And where is he from?"

"Frigarth."

30

Raiden

HERA, MOTHER OF ASSASSINS, turns narrowed eyes on me. "Is he, now?"

Zara grins, preening under this woman's attention. She's played me this entire time.

"And how did you end up with a man from Frigarth?"

"He's been searching for the lost princess." A hint of laughter rings in Zara's voice, the sound sending another stab through my heart.

Hera's face remains blank at Zara's words.

"He was the one who followed Kyler's mark."

"Ah," Hera finally says, turning back to Zara. "That situation was handled rather sloppily."

Zara turns her eyes down, chastised.

"I suppose we shouldn't be surprised this happened. But, perhaps we could learn from him."

My stomach clenches, but for now, Hera's attention is back on Zara. *Your princess*, I remind myself, despite the sharpness in my chest.

"Tell me about your missions."

Zara glances up, a smirk playing across her lips again.

"You've already heard about Mivaan?"

"Yes," Hera says. Her hair is absurdly long. "Air bubbles?"

Zara nods, eagerly. "They said it was his heart."

Air bubbles.

"Very good. How much did you use?" Her voice twists in curiosity. I could almost believe she was a normal woman, if it weren't for the cunning, the cruelty lighting those eyes.

"The full syringe. I didn't want to risk it not working."

Hera smiles. "Good. And Aeris?"

"Done," Zara says. I expect her eyes to flicker towards me, but she maintains the perfect lie.

At least her sister is safe. To betray Zara would be to betray Aeris, but the girl doesn't deserve that. I'll hold to this lie, too. Even if I can't make sense of it all.

"She fell into the sea, but my dagger was in her heart. That's when Elvar caught up with me."

"Ah, this is the soldier who arrested you?" Hera doesn't bother looking at me.

My eyebrows rise. Zara said Hera knew everything. But I'm still surprised. She must have spies in all the key cities and towns. Efficient. And a frightening prospect.

How many are in Frigarth watching my king and queen?

Zara merely nods again.

"Well done, Eilah," Hera says, fingering one of the knives at her belt. "Put him in the chair."

My heart thuds loudly in my chest. There's no way out. No one to help. And with no one else in the room, it's the Mother of Assassins herself about to see to my torture.

I hope I die before betraying Laurel and Turin.

As Zara leads me to the chair, a new thought enters my mind. I might not be able to bring any information back to the king and queen, but if I play my cards right, perhaps Hera will reveal hers.

After seventeen long years, I'll die knowing the truth.

I sit without struggling, the metal cold through my clothes. Zara straps my arms down with the chains dangling from the chair, so tightly the blood pounds in my hands. She tugs the gag down from my mouth. Her eyes remain empty, and I don't bother asking for her help.

With one last grin my way, she turns back to her mother.

"I imagine you just want to establish the basics. Darius asked me to help with the kids. I'll come back later?"

"That won't be necessary. It won't take long to learn what I need." Hera waves her hand vaguely. "We'll grab dinner later?"

"Absolutely."

Princess Zara, assassin, leaves me without so much as a backwards glance.

The door clicks shut behind her.

"You did a good job on her," I say, staring up into Hera's eyes.

Her head cocks. "I did, didn't I? But I suspect it's not her training you're talking about."

I suck in a deep breath.

"You thought I would lie?" Hera laughs, the sound sending a chill down my bones. "Not when I need to know what you know, and what you've told my daughter and her parents."

"I know everything. And so do Laurel and Turin."

"I doubt that," Hera purrs, stepping closer. "Or Eilah wouldn't be here right now."

I shrug or try to, but the chains stop me from moving. "I sent them a letter."

Her eyebrows raise. "That means little to me. They still have to find us."

I nod.

"And Eilah? Does she know?"

"No."

Hera's brow furrows. "First lie," she says, hand trailing to one of her many knives.

I pause. Zara's admonition that I can't act trailing through my mind. I need to mix in some truth. "I told her my theory that the princess was taken by you and your people to see how receptive she was to the idea."

"And?"

"I'm tied to a chair in the middle of the desert."

Hera laughs again, drawing her knife in one clean motion.

"That I might believe," she says, "if you weren't so willingly handing over the information."

"Self-preservation," I say. It's all about what to reveal and when.

"It's rather futile." She rests the tip of her knife on my forearm, the point pricking my skin. Her hair falls around her face in a thick curtain. She would be beautiful if not for the hatred claiming her soul.

"Why doesn't she remember?" I ask, ignoring the knife, refusing to give her the satisfaction of acknowledging it.

Hera's head tilts. "Because I made it so," she whispers, dragging the knife along my arm.

I grunt but keep my eyes glued to hers as warmth seeps through my shirt sleeves.

"She said you didn't have powers."

"You really think I could have all this with no magic?" She spreads her arms. "You *really* think the sister of the greatest shapeshifter this world has ever seen is magicless?" Hera's voice is hard, admonition in it.

"No," I murmur, mentally berating myself for ever thinking it could be true. "So why does she?"

"They all think that," she smirks. "My magic works without a trace. And if anyone realises ... well they don't remember."

"Memory magic?"

She nods. No wonder she doesn't care what she tells me.

"Then why are we talking?"

She laughs. "Because it's so much easier to ask. You want me to sift through all those memories to find what I need to know?"

No. No, I don't want that. But I also don't want her to think I have something to hide. "It would be efficient."

"I like you," she says, now resting the knife on my thigh. "But you're right. I can't risk Eilah knowing." Her eyes turn thoughtful. "I could make her forget all about you."

I can't help it. My eyes widen.

"Oh," she tsks, "but what's this? Did you lie to me again?"

I shake my head, heart pounding at the slip. If Zara forgets me ... she could forget who she is. And then there will be no hope for her to get home. Even if she doesn't believe it now.

She *can't* forget me.

The knife slips into my skin.

"What is this?" Hera repeats, her tone turning cold. "Why don't you want her to forget?"

I grit my teeth, mind racing. A truth. A truth to use as a lie.

"I love her," the words burst from my mouth.

Hera recoils as the words echo in the room, the knife goes with her.

"Love?"

I swallow, nodding. Blood trickles down my arm and leg.

Hera throws back her head and cackles.

"Oh, this is too good! You have feelings for my daughter, the girl who doesn't believe in love! The girl who killed the first boy she ever liked! And here you are, dying at my hand."

Sorren. The boy who tried to kill her.

"Enough," I growl.

"Enough?" Hera snaps bone-chillingly fast to her cold self, her eyebrow rising. "Yes, I think it is."

She leans forwards, clamping her hand down upon my injured arm. I grunt. And her knife comes to rest at my throat.

31

Zara

"**S**HALL I PASS ON your love declaration to *my* daughter?"

I barely hear her words over the echo of Raiden's in my mind. *I love her.*

He can't act, I remind myself as my mind moves to dismiss his words.

Fool.

Idiot.

But mine.

I stare through the little hole in the floor. This little place has been my secret since I was a child. When Mother wouldn't let me sit in on questionings, I would sneak up here to her abandoned library, and watch from above. Determined to force my stomach to stop turning at the thought of hurting, of killing someone, I would make myself watching it all. *Hear* it all. Imagining it was some kind of game, the first of many. A way to stop my stomach from churning, from the bile rising in my throat at the thought of the pain and deaths I had caused and would continue to cause.

And she just admitted everything to Raiden.

He was right.

"I think she already knows," Raiden murmurs, so low I almost miss it.

I wouldn't mind hearing it again, I think, as I continue pulling and stretching my magic. The ghost of our kiss lingers on my lips. The softness of his, and the tenderness of his hand in my hair.

The circle forming around me grows, sharpens. I'm not sure this will work, but it has too. I yank harder on the magic, drawing it up as quickly as I can now, a rush in my veins.

"Very well," Mother says.

I raise my arms, and the ice follows, and then I slam it down.

The wooden floor below me gives way in a perfect circle, cut cleanly by the sharp edges of the ice. I plummet down, letting my magic flow out of the ice as we fall two meters. It shatters as it slams into the ground.

I roll as I hit the floor, shards of ice cutting my skin, and push to my feet, one steel dagger ready in my palm.

"Eilah," Hera sighs, glancing over Raiden's shoulder at me as if this is just another ordinary day. He's between us now, my back to the locked door.

My hand twists, palm angled towards Raiden, low and out of sight from her.

"Actually," I say. "It's Zara."

Raiden's form stiffens.

"Get out of here!" he shouts.

I roll my eyes, and stand my ground.

"I know too much now for her to make me forget," I say, infusing a confidence I don't feel into my words. I have no idea the depths of her magic. I had no idea she *had* magic. "Right, Mother?"

"Actually," Hera purrs. "Not exactly."

Something slams into my mind, and my body jolts, the room spinning as everything slowly goes dark

The soldier's blue eyes follow me. The world blurs and suddenly the tall, muscular man is in front of me.

"You can't seem to get your eyes off me, soldier. Perhaps you'd like to dance?"

His hand is clasped in mine, the other cupping my waist.

"Raiden. Raiden Elvar."

"A pleasure," I purr. The music runs over itself and suddenly I'm angry.

"Whoever you're looking for is dead, soldier. We're assassins," I hiss.

"Now be a gentleman and leave me alone." I push away from him, careening into another man, air pouring into his veins.

I don't remember leaving the party or sleeping, but it's morning and I'm leaving the city far behind me on the back of a mare.

The soldier is before me again. "Deliah!" *he snaps, tugging the mare's reins.*

"Be grateful I've let you live this long, soldier. I have places to be, people to kill. Now, be a good little soldier, and go home." *I grin pouring as much of my rage into it as I can muster.* "Maybe I'll even see you there one day soon."

He's leaning over me in the dark, concern in his eyes. Pain radiates across my shoulder.

"Making sure you were still alive. You've gone two minutes without insulting me. I was worried."

What is he talking about?

"Guess you needed that distraction after all."

He pulls me upwards, eyes and hands trailing over my back. "Zara?"

"Ah, I see. The birthmark. We'll have to fix that."

What? What was that?

Image after image, nothing more than flashes of colour go by but always a voice seeps through.

"It's my duty to protect you, Your Highness. I go where you go. Your battle is my battle."

"Let me help."

Colours whirl fast, too quickly for me to lock onto anything.

"I'm glad you saved her."

The same one. Always.

"I have no delusions about what you are, Princess."

"Don't go back to her."

And I know it.

"I wouldn't need weapons to stop you."

"I'll never lie to you."

"They've suffered enough."

"I don't look that old!"

I know. I know.

"You didn't deny it."

"I may have only paid half."

"I'm not leaving you again."

"Let me help you."

"I'm going to try something. And I would greatly appreciate it if you didn't stab me."

I know him.

Your battles are my battles.

"Zara!"

Raiden.

This time when the world jolts, it rightens. The room appears before my eyes again as my body starts to fall. I catch myself against the back of the empty chair.

Empty.

I shake my head, trying to pull myself together, fighting the sluggishness that pulls at my mind, threatening to drag me under.

Raiden and Hera are sprawled on the ground, my shadow's legs still awkwardly tied together. But the chains hang from the chair, frozen and snapped off.

It's Raiden's grunt of pain that finally brings me back to myself, that finally makes my legs straighten and my body move as terror laces through me. He doesn't stand a chance against Hera.

She has a knife.

I dive forwards, sliding across the rough wooden floor, grabbing Hera's hand and slamming it into the ground. I pump my magic into her as I do, watching as ice forms on her skin. The knife goes flying. But she has so many more on her body.

"Move," I shout, shoving Raiden aside with my body. I've no idea what injuries he's sustained.

Hera shrieks, slipping her body out from underneath us as Raiden and I try to swap places. My hand still grips hers, ice fusing her flesh to mine.

Her feet are under her in an instant, even as I slam my hip into hers and try to throw her forwards.

She regains her balance before I can complete the move.

"Enough of this, Eilah!" she snaps, her fist shooting for my throat.

I duck, sending my own into her ribs.

Raiden tries to jump back in, crimson flashing on his skin, but I send a backwards kick into his chest, sending him flying.

"In fighting now, dear?" Hera croons, preparing to throw her knife after him.

I yank on her hair, and her throw goes off, sending the weapon into the wall.

We're a tangle of limbs, moving equally fast, using the same moves, knowing instinctively what the other will do. We can't gain ground on each other. And a part of me is proud.

Hera, Mother of Assassins, can't get the upper hand.

Until she does.

In a flash I'm on the floor, another weapon pressed to my throat, her feet tangled in mine.

But that's not all that keeps be still.

My hair is caught under her knee. Exactly as she planned.

"Now," Hera purrs, and my skin prickles under her blade. My mind threatens to jump back to the Cutting, but I force myself to focus under the familiar experience. "This is all a big mistake, darling. There's no need to fight."

"No?" I spit, struggling.

"Just stay still and things will be back to normal in a moment," she says, through gritted teeth. The mother that greeted me minutes earlier is gone, her eyes hard with fury.

Where is Raiden?

"I'm done working for you," I growl.

"You're done when I say you're done," Hera says, leaning closer, face inches from mine. "And you won't be done until I've had my revenge for Lily. For my flower."

I swallow, sending the blade deeper into my skin. Ignoring the way my traitorous heart races in my chest, I fix my eyes on hers.

"I saw them," I whisper.

Nothing flickers in eyes.

"You went to Frigarth without orders?" Her knife presses harder. "Another step, soldier, and I end her."

"Don't hurt her!" Raiden puffs.

I can't twist to see him, but I know his eyes are on me.

My hand is still stuck to Hera's, but I haven't used any more magic up until now. It's been a long time since I reached the end of it, since I grew too tired to twist more of it. And breaking through the floor required immense concentration.

And what I need to do would require a lot of magic. It would have to be fast. It would have to be complete.

And then I'd still need to get out of here.

It's that last step that seems too impossible, but in that moment, I throw rule number two away. Forsake the idea of my escape. Because it's not only me here.

"It was his voice," I whisper, tugging harder at the thread of magic within me.

"Whose? The soldier?" Hera asks, frowning down at me.

"No, my father's."

Her eyes widen, then she laughs. "A weak spot in the magic! Never mind, that can be fixed."

I close my eyes, keeping myself only half present as I try to tell my magic what I'll need. I can feel it, coaxed under my mental fingers, readying. Eager.

"Will things go back to the way they were?" I ask.

"Of course," Hera says, her voice twisting in false kindness.

"OK," I whisper, injecting as much defeat into my voice as I can. "I'll come willingly. But I want Elvar alive. He can help the trainers."

Mother laughs, her breath against my skin.

"You think he's going to help train us?"

"Yes. For me, he would."

"Zara!" he gasps.

The knife at my throat presses deeper.

"You will!" I grunt.

"Open your eyes, Eilah," Hera snaps.

"No." Because I can't contain this much longer, and the magic will show in my eyes. It's happened before, I've been told. And this close, she won't miss it.

I let my body relax under her. Defeated. Every nerve in my body screams to fight. I make my voice drop.

"Please."

"Zara!" Raiden grunts, his voice close enough that I know Mother could kill him and still have me trapped below her.

"It's Eilah," I murmur.

Just another moment, I tell the magic, the ice making my veins run cold.

The knife wavers, pulls away barely a millimeter.

"Good," Mother says. "This will be over in a moment."

"Yes." I open my eyes. "It will."

The magic shoots out of every part of my body in contact with Mother. My hand still iced to hers, my leg resting against hers, my ankles tangled in her feet. My torso where she sits on me. Ice shoots across her skin, her flesh, swallowing her. Her eyes widen and she pulls back, mouth opening in terror, but I tell the magic to hurry, feel the energy draining out of me as if it's the magic itself.

She's screaming, Raiden is shouting, and I can do nothing but watch as I'm pinned below her, urging the ice on and on and on. Begging it to be quick. To freeze all of her.

Until it's over.

There's a long pause, as though the world takes a deep breath.

"Zara?" Raiden gasps, and I hear him stumbling forwards.

"Yeah?" I mumble, vision spotting as my head spins.

His face appears over me, next to what could be the perfect sculpture of mother. His mouth opens and closes, lost for words. Again.

I cough a laugh, then groan at the way the world spins harder, the ache in my head.

"Are you all right?"

"No," I moan. "And I'm stuck."

"Good, because there's something I need to say." His eyes soften, then harden as he stares down at me.

"WHAT THE HELL WAS THAT?"

"Help now, yell later."

"I can't believe that was all an act!" he shouts, but I can tell he's not truly angry. His brow isn't as furrowed as it would be. And his eyes aren't nearly as crinkled. An open book, as usual, and I could never tire of reading him.

"I told you," I say, closing my eyes against the whirling, "you're a terrible actor."

"I—" He laughs in disbelief. "And you, you are amazing."

I open my eyes, fighting a smile. "Help now, compliment later."

"Right." His hand rises but then he stops. "How?"

I swallow. I'm not sure. I think we're frozen together. And I might have been able to separate us, but I'm not sure my body could take more magic right now.

I tell him as much in a low voice. It's almost an admission of weakness, but he says nothing to make me feel bad, merely nodding and studying the points that connect us more closely.

"We'll have to cut your hair."

Shouts erupt from outside all around us, and from inside the tower itself. Then comes the clash of steel on steel.

"What's happening?" I squirm but can't gain an inch. The ice creaks above me. I stop, eyes widening. I don't think I could stand breaking her.

Raiden jumps to his feet—slower than usual—and awkwardly shuffles to the window.

"It's—the assassins are fighting each other."

"What?"

"Some are trying to come this way."

My mind races despite the exhaustion. "She must have affected some of their memories too. When she died, the magic released."

There is no change in me, because I already had my memories back. But they didn't.

And now some want to leave, and the more loyal members will kill them. Some will come here for Mother, and some for me—to take my place as Hera's heir.

"We need to get out of here, Raiden," I say, urgently.

"There's a bird coming ...?"

"A hawk?" I try to tilt my head but I can't see the window.

"Yes."

"Let her in." I hope I won't regret this. "Pick up Hera's dagger, but don't hurt her unless she attacks."

He does as I say, stooping to cut his legs free, and sending me a shooting glance but I say nothing.

Hope is rising in my chest, but fear is equally strong. What happens if she—

The hawk flies into the room, shifting in midair, and Nina nimbly drops to the ground.

"Eilah! Eilah? What is going on?" she gushes, and then a gasp sounds. "Mother?"

"Nina, Nina, please listen." I mentally shove at the ache in my head in frustration. "Mother's been lying, she's been blocking memories, and she tried to kill us."

There's a moment of silence, then, "I know. She took things from me too."

Relief washes over me.

"I'm sorry."

"Who's this?" Nina asks, her voice turning cheekily suspicious despite everything.

"My shadow."

"Raiden Elvar."

There's a beat of silence.

"Can someone please get me out of here?"

Raiden hurries forwards, knife gripped in his bloody hand. "I have to cut your hair."

My mouth drops open, but then a spool of satisfaction forms in my stomach at the thought. "Good."

"How are we going to get you out?" Nina asks, dropping to her knees on my other side. Her hair is longer than the last time I saw her. That absurd thought is the first thing that crosses my mind.

"Darius said you haven't been on a mission yet," I say, panic settling in. She hasn't gone out yet, has she?

Nina shakes her head, as I notice Raiden trying to gather my hair.

"Not yet, but I was finally entering the next stage." Her eyes fill with tears of relief. "Thank you. Thank you for stopping her."

Raiden clears his throat. "Ready?"

"Go for it."

Even though I'm lying down, I can feel the moment the hair is cut free, somewhere around my shoulders. And with it, a weight inside my soul falls away too. I almost wish for him to cut more.

"We might have to break her," Raiden says quietly, studying the ice.

Bile forms in my throat at the thought. It won't be pretty. Not that that's ever been an issue for me before. But even though Hera isn't my mother, she's still ... my mother.

"Let me try wriggling first." Now that I can also move my head, it's easier to shift around.

"Can't you use your magic?" Nina asks, her frown audible.

"No," I say, trying to force the ice free. "I used too much."

"How? This is nothing." Nina scrunches her face, beyond puzzled.

I pause, glancing her way. "It's not a lot of ice, but the concentration, the skill ... It was a lot."

"Oh."

"She also broke through the ceiling," Raiden adds, impressed.

Nina might know a little of how magic works because of her shifted form, but she's never had to worry about using too much. She's never had the sense of a vague line that she can't cross, one that takes more energy the closer you get to it. A line I am so very dangerously close to.

Mother would have been proud if it wasn't her I did it too.

The thought actually turns my stomach.

Raiden grabs the hand that is still stuck to mine and carefully wriggles it. I can feel the ice moving, space appearing between us. Nina does the same with one of Hera's feet.

It's an absurd situation.

The clangs from outside grow louder, echoing in the room.

"What's happening out there?" I ask Nina, still wriggling.

"Brooks," Nina says grimly. "One of the younger ones must have remembered something, because suddenly he was furious and trying to get away. And Brooks killed him for being a traitor. He's trying to rally everyone against whoever tries to leave. He said if Mother made us forget something, then we were already traitors."

Great.

Their movements grow faster.

"Pull your hand free." Raiden moves down to help Nina. Hera's thumb is the main problem, curled around the back of my hand, it restricts my movements. But I manage to twist and slide in the precious space Raiden has made. Her frozen fingers graze my skin—twinging the places raw from her tight grip—but my hand is now free.

But now I can't do anything other than wait for my legs to come free.

"Hurrying?"

"I'm trying," Nina grunts. Raiden says nothing. But the sounds from outside are growing louder. Smoke now wafts through the window. Only a fire wielder could light this place on fire.

But is he on our side or theirs?

I can't wait any longer.

Bracing my hands beneath me, I try to shimmy out from underneath Mother, dragging my body up along the floor. My skin pulls tight, ice grates, but I gain half an inch.

"Wait!" Raiden says. "You'll hurt yourself."

"There's no time," I snap. "Once they get in here, we're dead. Or I am, since you can both fly out of here." I pause. "You should both get out of here."

I keep shimmying, ignoring the way my skin starts to tear on my legs, my feet, and my abdomen.

"I told you, I'm not leaving you," Raiden growls, and the pressure eases on my legs as he tugs on Hera's. I ignore the way my stomach twists with guilt, and the warmth that threatens to rise in my chest.

Nina says nothing, but I imagine her frown is as deep as Raiden's. Forget the shadow, how did I end up with such a stubborn sister?

Actually, I don't want to know.

"Then grab one of her legs and pull up," I grunt.

I can feel the moment she joins Raiden's efforts, my hips come free and then I slide out from underneath Mother.

"Are you OK?" Nina dives on top of me, and the air leaves my lungs in a whoosh. The ache in my head doubles and I have to close my eyes to the way the room spins. But my sister in my arms makes it all better.

"Yes."

I didn't realise how much I needed Nina to be with me. To support me.

I slap her back before I can linger there too long. "We need to go."

While she's clambering to her feet, Raiden grabs my hand and hauls me upright. I stumble, the world still off-kilter, but his hands steady me.

"OK?" His eyes study me, hold mine.

I nod, breaking eye contact and huffing.

I have to be.

"Good," he says, unsheathing one of my daggers and pushing the hilt into my hand. He hangs onto Hera's.

I whirl on Nina.

"If you're staying with us, I have one rule."

She bristles but nods.

"You have to stay with him." I point at Raiden.

Indignant noises come from them both, each thinking they're the one being told they need to be protected. I can't say I really care, because they're both right.

"Enough," I snap at them both. "It's either that or I throw you both out the window."

Raiden laughs, and it takes all my concentration to maintain the glare I level his way. The sounds of his humour echoes in my ears.

He sobers.

"Can we just go?" Nina sighs, shifting on her feet.

I hurry to the window, keeping my body away from the frame and carefully peer around. War has broken out in the compound, and not an inch of it is untouched.

Brothers and sisters fight in the main training grounds, weapons and magic a flurry of motion exactly as before, but now the blood that soaks the sand is permanent. The younger ones, some as little as five, are huddled in groups, fighting in groups, or running in groups. At least they know to keep together. And Brooks is at the centre of it all, fighting his way through the bodies, cutting down each sibling that comes for him.

Something pangs in my chest.

He might not be the best, but he *is* good.

"Raiden, your swords are on the landing."

It was a good place at the time to leave them, but now ... I hope no one's out there yet.

"We need to get to the stables. We'll at least need a camel to get out of here." Preferably two, but both of them can fly if worse comes to worse.

"What about food? Water?" Nina asks.

"We'll find it on the way." On the way to the stables, or on the way through the desert. One will be a much better experience than the other.

Without another word, I stride across the room and yank open the door.

There's no one there.

Throwing Raiden his swords, I wait barely a moment for him and Nina to join me before starting down the stairs.

32

Zara

MOTHER FOLLOWED THE CLASSIC design for the tower, so anyone coming up the stairs is more exposed than those coming down due to the curve of the stairs. Which means I have a better chance of killing whoever comes up, than they do of me.

The question is, which of my siblings is dumb enough to try to kill me in here?

We reach the second floor without seeing anyone. Nina grabs my shoulder before I can go any further.

"They'll be waiting."

"Yep," I say. I wish I could see where Brooks is, but I can hardly stay here and wait for him like a cornered animal.

I take the steps, and race down, determined to catch any-one waiting for me by surprise.

A sword slashes through the air, barely missing my face. I duck instinctively and roll, gaining precious space.

And the move puts my assailant right in the middle of my group, with me on one side and Raiden and Nina on the other. He's dispatched in seconds.

No one else has made it into the tower, and I flatten my back against the stone wall beside the open door, and glance outside.

The grounds are thick with fighting, but there's no sign of Brooks yet. He can't be far. He won't miss an opportunity to kill me.

Something presses against my back, and I don't have to look to know it's Raiden.

"What's wrong?" he whispers.

"Nothing," I say, trying to ignore his closeness. His warmth. "Looking for my brother."

"He'll try to kill her," Nina adds helpfully.

"Nina!"

"Brooks?" Raiden asks, his voice darkening.

I *knew* he heard all that.

"Nothing I can't handle, even like this," I say with more confidence than I feel. I could kill him in an instant if my magic wasn't so hard to reach right now. But it just means I'll have to be careful, time my attacks. If I do it right, I'll only need my magic once.

I don't wait for him to reply, but dive through the door. Raiden and Nina are close behind, one on either side of me. I push us into a jog, heading for the stables. Brooks will find me, no matter where I go, so we might as well head in the right direction.

We round the boy's dormitory and I stumble in my steps. Brooks stands before me, sword drawn and already dripping crimson. And in front of him are two of our youngest siblings, barely five years old. He takes a step towards them. Rage sets a fire in my belly.

"Brooks!" I scream, hand gripping my dagger so hard I'm surprised the hilt doesn't break.

"Eilah!" Nina gasps.

"Get those kids to the stables. I'll meet you both there."

Brooks whirls around, his face twisting in a dark smile.

"Zara—"

"Now, Raiden." My tone leaves no room for argument.

I take his heavy silence as agreement and pace away in an arc, eyes never leaving Brooks's silver ones. He mirrors my movements, leaving the children forgotten.

"You stop me from killing traitors, sister," Brooks says, cocking his head. "I thought you would be the champion of this cause."

I shake my head. "We don't kill children."

Brooks chuckles. "But that's not it, is it?"

His eyes widen as though a thought has just occurred to him, and he glances at the tower.

Nina and Raiden dart behind me, racing for the kids.

"She's not coming," I confirm, forcing my face to twist into a smirk. I need his attention solely on me. And I've always found rage to be a good motivator.

Raiden scoops up both the children in his arms, and the four of them disappear around the corner. Something eases inside me, but I force myself to focus.

Brooks's face darkens. "Is she all right?"

I pause, then laugh. He doesn't think I could have done it. Perhaps didn't think I would try. She was my mother after all.

"She's dead, brother." I slowly pull my other dagger free, holding it backwards in my grip.

"What?" he whispers, the tip of his sword wobbling, a break in his armour.

"She lied. Lied about everything. Did you know, I'm not even her daughter?"

Brooks stares at me for a long moment and I let him, let Raiden and Nina get further away. Let my magic recover bit by bit.

"You killed her?" his voice shakes.

"Yes, that's what I said."

He roars, actually roars, and races towards me.

I twist my face into a grin, and raise my daggers.

I duck his first swing, and his second, and his third.

He growls, whirling to face me, splatters of blood on his skin shine in the sun.

But I dodge his blow again.

"Fight me!" he yells, and I hear an echo of myself in his words.

Don't I owe—shudder—him the chance to change? To realise the lives we've both lived have been for nothing but revenge over a conflict we started?

"Brooks," I pant, dodging another swipe of his sword. My head spins, but I keep my feet firm under me. "Stop this."

"You killed her!" he repeats, his foot coming for my face. I sway backwards, watching his boot pass within a centimeter of my nose.

"Why do you care? She wasn't your mother. She stole you, like she did nearly everyone here."

It's a fact we've all known, and all ignored. Some have come of their own will, but most, most of us were taken.

I suppose with Mother's mind magic ... maybe we were *all* taken. We just handled it differently, and some had to forget.

"I was nothing before. Nothing."

"You've killed for her. For her revenge," I shout.

"And I enjoyed it, as you did," he spits as his fist connects with my jaw.

I stumble back, barely parrying the tip of his sword darting for my chest.

I wonder if he knows it's his words that hurt more than anything he could do to me, because he's right. I did enjoy it. I really, really did.

I sigh, a move hard around the panting of my breaths, and try one last time.

"Things don't have to go this way. We can walk away."

Brooks stops, a meter all that separates us. "Except I don't want to. With Mother gone and you following her, someone needs to run this place."

"Oh, Brooks," I say, finally raising my daggers, "you were not made to be in charge."

I meet him blow for blow, deflecting his moves along my dagger, keeping as much of the brunt off my aching body as possible. I send darting attacks his way only when there are openings, never risking much. I need to end this soon, before he questions why I haven't used my magic. But I also need to conserve my energy. It's a delicate balance.

One I can't maintain.

Brooks's eyes narrow.

"What's this?" he asks, twisting to let my dagger slide harmlessly past him. His eyes study mine. "You've used too much haven't you?"

My stomach drops but I keep my face blank.

It doesn't matter. He grins.

"I should have known the moment you didn't cut me down with a storm of ice," he says, grin widening.

He throws his head forwards, slamming into my face. I stumble back, whipping a dagger in front of me as he follows, opening a deep cut across his chest.

Blood flows from my eyebrow into my eye.

I furiously wipe my face, as my brother stalks towards me.

He thinks I can't use magic. And maybe that's not such a bad thing.

Because I've got just a little bit left. And now his guard is down.

I dive forwards, slashing for the hand gripping his sword.

Get inside his range, cripple him.

He turns his wrist at the last possible moment and my blade only grazes his forearm. I whirl, sending my elbow flying towards his face. He catches it, but the force still sends his hand crashing into his own face. I laugh, grabbing his sword hand before he can move, and slam my heel hard into his foot.

He stumbles back and I throw myself forwards into a roll.

A sharp pain erupts across my back, and sand sticks to my skin. The world rightens, but my head continues to spin. I need to end this, and soon.

I twist, my own blood now dripping from Brooks's blade.

"That's the last drop you take," I promise.

"You have no magic," he says, throwing his arms wide, a glint in his eyes.

"That's never stopped me before," I scoff, "or have you forgotten our sparring matches?"

I smirk at the way his face darkens and race at him. Before he can raise his sword, I leap into the air, bringing my foot around to come slamming into his jaw. But my balance is off, my jolting vision throwing my aim, and the kick lands against his shoulder. He stumbles, but the move is far less effective than I'd hoped.

I follow through with a jab to his chin, using the hilt of my dagger. His head flies back. But his hand grabs my arm and a jolt flies through my skin, opening my hand against my will. My dagger drops uselessly to the ground.

"You've learned a new trick," I say, twisting my arm and ripping it free of his grip. My hand still tingles in the wake of his magic.

"No," he grunts, spittles of blood flying from his mouth from where he's bitten his lip. "I've been saving this one."

My eyes widen in surprise, but I don't get a moment to think on it as he plants his foot against my abdomen and shoves me backwards.

As though in slow motion, I watch his sword come around, soaring for me. And his guard is open. The last dregs of my magic rises, tugged and coerced to sit just under my skin before we'd even started fighting, and I throw one, small, crooked and melting ice dagger for his heart.

His blade slices through my skin, and my dagger finds its home.

And the world slips away.

I'm awake before a minute has passed, the blood pounding in my ears, the fighting around me nothing more than a faint and dull noise.

I struggle to push my shaking arms under me, raising my head enough to see Brooks's unmoving, bloodied, body.

I let my head fall back into the sand, and tentatively reach a hand towards my abdomen. Warmth coats it.

I was an idiot to use so much magic on Mother, and now I'm defenceless, weak, and barely able to move. In the middle of a compound full of assassins.

I just hope Raiden and Nina are still alive.

Kneel or fight.

Fight, always. Even when it's hard.

Groaning, I push myself to my feet, one arm hugging my body.

I close my eyes to the spinning, the pounding, force air deep into my lungs, and push myself on.

Kneel or fight.

I keep my arm tucked against my abdomen. It's not immediately life-threatening. A life of fighting in these grounds has taught me that much. But it needs cleaning and stitching—or healing.

But I'm not about to trust one of my brothers or sisters.

The stables aren't far. Down past the end of the boy's dormitory, then a straight shot down the north wall. Raiden and Nina will be there. Waiting. I can't allow myself to think of the alternative.

I stumble into the boy's dormitory.

My eyes take a moment to adjust but I don't linger in the doorway where my silhouette can easily be seen.

I edge along the inside wall until the dark spots clear and the room opens up before me. Empty. Thank goodness. I hurry to the nearest bunk bed and tear open the drawers beside it.

I have no medical supplies left in my backpack, and I'm not even sure if Raiden still has it.

A strip of fabric, a headscarf, lies in the first drawer and I grab it, tying it roughly around my abdomen. The pressure sends me gasping, but the wound is covered and protected, and the blood flow should slow.

I keep digging.

"Hey!"

I jolt, whirling towards the voice, one hand still in the drawer.

But I left my daggers outside.

Idiot.

"Eilah?"

I squint at the figure in the doorway, the light framing him also keeping me from seeing his face. But I know that voice.

"Darius?"

"What are you doing?" he says, voice cautious as he edges inside, copying my earlier movements and standing against the wall.

I swallow, glancing at the weapon in his hand.

"Leave me be," I say, pushing as much warning as I can into the words. We've always gotten along before. Surely he remembers that.

He hesitates.

"Did you kill Brooks?"

"Yes," I say, slowly rifling inside the draw. Surely one of these boys keeps a weapon here.

"And your mother?

"Her, too."

Darius merely nods. I can't tell what he's thinking, and I hate it. I hate that my brother has had the same training I have. But I don't hide my feelings from him, not this time.

"Let me pass, Darius. I don't want to kill you." I swallow heavily.

"I don't think you could," he murmurs. "Did you know you're swaying?"

I raise my chin as my hand clenches on the handle of the smallest knife imaginable.

Outside, a rook caws.

Hope swells in my chest. "What will it be, brother?"

His hand raises, his mouth opening, right as the rook swoops in. He transforms in an instant, slamming Darius into the wall. My brother sprawls to the ground unconscious.

"Don't kill him!" I yell at my shadow standing over him, swords drawn.

He huffs, giving me a look. "I wasn't going to."

"Just making sure." I pull the knife out of the drawers and sigh at the size of it. Still, I suppose it's better than nothing.

"What happened?" The voice comes from right in front of me, and fingers skim the fabric at my abdomen.

I jump, instinctively shoving him away. "Don't do that!"

His eyebrows rise, but the concern in his eyes deepens. "I didn't know it was possible to sneak up on an assassin."

I don't deign to respond, turning to search the next drawer.

"How's Nina?"

"She's fine. What are you looking for, Zara?" Raiden asks, quietly.

"I need a needle and thread."

"Don't you have an infirmary?" Raiden asks, ducking over to the next set of drawers.

"We do, but I'd rather not fight my way over there. Would you?"

He says nothing, and in the silence the guilt rises in me again. I shove it away. I didn't truly betray him, and he knows that. So why do I feel bad?

I slam the drawer closed, stumbling as I do.

"Zara?"

"I'm fine," I grunt.

"Lie on the bed."

"What?" I whirl, wincing at the movement.

"I found what you're searching for." Raiden holds up the thread.

257

"Oh."

It's two steps, but it could almost be a mile as I stumble over, more falling onto the mattress than anything else.

Raiden appears by my side, kneeling on the ground so he can lean under the top bunk. He's facing the door, but if someone did come in, we'd both be at a significant disadvantage.

Somehow, I don't think he cares.

"We really need to clean it," Raiden says, pulling me from my thoughts.

"This is to get us out of here. There are plenty of plants in the desert I can use for that," I say, waving aside his concern.

Raiden's brow crinkles, but he nods. Carefully, he pulls a long thread free from a ruined cotton shirt and threads it through the needle. His hand is steady despite the cut to his arm. I wonder what other wounds he's gained.

I raise my hands to remove the headscarf from my abdomen, and hope he doesn't notice the way my hands are shaking. It's been a long time since I've used this much magic. And I don't want to do it again for a long, long time.

He gently bats my hands away. "Let me do that."

I huff.

"This is oddly familiar," he says, carefully pulling the fabric away. I ignore the way it sticks to my skin.

"Not quite," I say, trying to lighten the mood. Because maybe that guilt hasn't gone away yet. "I haven't threatened to kill you."

His lips quirk for a moment. "No, but you did nearly carry through on the threat. Again."

I stare at the underside of the top bunk.

"I wasn't going to let her do anything to you."

"I know." He pauses. "I may have doubted it at the time. But I know."

"Your arm ..." I murmur, catching sight of the blood again.

"It's nothing," he says, not even glancing at it. He tears the shirt around my wound, leaving it open to the warm air. Guess I'll need a new combat suit.

Or maybe, maybe I don't. There's no one to work for now. No one to kill for.

I wince as Raiden's fingers travel along the edges of the wound.

"Sorry," he hums. "I don't like the idea of sewing this up."

"It'll be fine," I grunt. "Get on with it."

"You have a terrible bedside manner. I'm glad I'm not the one needing stitches."

The needle pricks my skin without warning, and I suck in a breath.

"Trying to distract me again?" I say around gritted teeth.

"Mmm," he says, "worked last time."

I turn my head to look up at him, watching the way his eyes focus on my skin, the way his brow turns in a frown. My fingers ache with the desire to turn him towards me, to rest on his face.

"I'm sorry."

"What for?" he says, eyes flicking to mine briefly. But he continues patching me up.

"For poisoning you and handing you over to her," I whisper, watching him intently, desperately wanting those eyes on me again.

He's silent for a long moment, so long I wonder if he's going to say anything back. My stomach twists. He promised he'd never leave me ...

"You did say I'm a terrible actor."

"It's true," I say. I swallow, hating the way the words stick in my throat. "I'm still sorry."

"You haven't said that before, have you?" He grins, eyes flicking back to mine, and I know he's OK. We're OK.

"Raiden." I barely stop myself from slapping his arm.

His grin widens. "You've not said that much either. I could get used to hearing it more."

I laugh, glancing away. *I could get used to saying it.*

I lay there in silence, regulating my breathing as he continues to work his way along the wound. I haven't checked it out properly, but I can tell it's long. Perhaps a little deeper than I would prefer. But I'll be OK once I can clean it.

"All done," Raiden says, carefully tying the headscarf back in place.

"Thank you," I say, gingerly sitting up.

His mouth opens.

"Don't say it!" I laugh, clapping my hand over his mouth.

His eyes sparkle. "I wasn' 'oing to 'ay anyth—" he says through my hand.

I give him a pointed look.

He gently pulls my hand away.

"Where to next?"

"The stables."

"After that." He still hasn't let my hand go.

I know what he wants to hear. But I can't say it. I can't.

"The desert."

"Zara ..." He squeezes my hand.

"I don't know," I finally whisper, unable to turn away from him again. War raging inside me.

"You could come home," he says, tenderly pushing a strand of my newly shortened hair from my face. It's barely past my shoulders now, it'll take some getting used to, but I like it.

"Could I?" Could I really after everything I've done? I study the ring still on my finger. Lily's ring. The woman who killed their prince. My uncle. Two people who I have never even met, whose lives and deaths have determined my own.

It's a fitting heirloom when all I have done is follow in her footsteps.

Raiden's rough fingers tenderly tilt my head back up so I have to look at him.

"Always."

"I'm an assassin, Raiden." I hate how weak I sound, how lost and hurt and unsure.

But he doesn't care. And I think I don't hate him for that.

"You're a princess."

I shake my head.

"That doesn't change anything."

"No," he says, thoughtfully, "but *you* can. You can change it."

I can't say anything, not around the lump in my throat and the question I can't quite get past my lips.

"What is it?" Raiden asks, eyes searching mine, thumb absently stroking my cheek.

"Will you—" I clear my throat. "Will you still stay with me, shadow?"

His eyes positively shine. "Yes."

The memory of his lips on mine plays before my eyes.

"I—I don't think I can give you what you want. Not yet," I say gently, unsure if I want to see the pain form in his eyes.

But he smiles. "I never thought it would be that easy. But perhaps I can help you along the way."

I frown.

"I can remind you who you are, and who I'm not." Sorren's name hovers over his lips but he doesn't say it. "I can help you believe again, little by little."

"I think I would like that," I whisper. *I really, really would.*

I slide Aunt Lily's ring from my finger, and leave it on the bed. I don't think I'll be needing it anymore.

33

Raiden

"Zara!" I call, stepping through the light curtain surrounding the building we've been staying in. The entrance and attached rooms are empty. "Nina?"

"We're here!" Nina's bright voice calls from the other side of the small building. I stride forwards, wishing we didn't need so many curtains, but Zara had insisted on the privacy from outside.

I push through their curtain. Nina wouldn't have called out if they didn't want me in there.

Zara lies sprawled on her bed, her sister sitting on the edge beside her.

"Hello, assassin."

"Hello, shadow," she says lazily, an arm thrown over her eyes.

"It's time."

Zara jolts upright, and I smother a smirk. She's a tough assassin until any mention of her parents. At least she no longer loses all colour.

"Already?"

"Yes," I say patiently, leaning against a pillar.

Nina looks down at her sister. "Told you, you should have gotten changed."

"What's wrong with this?" Zara asks, glancing at her utilitarian pants and shirt, and the jacket she's worn for the past two days. "It's got lots of pockets."

"It smells, *Princess,*" Nina grunts.

The girl had accepted Zara's true position quickly, though with lots of excited squeals. My ears still haven't stopped ringing. But something had eased in Zara at the love of her sister.

"Fine." Zara shoves Nina from the bed and strips off the jacket.

Shaking my head, I smile, "They won't care what you're wearing."

"Right," Zara says, rubbing her hands together. There was a time where she wouldn't have let me see her so nervous. My heart warms a little, my eyes unable to leave her.

"Ready?" I ask. I'm not going to make her go if she's not ready. We can stay here as long as she needs. But I also think Laurel and Turin will tear the city apart if they don't see her soon.

"Yeah," she says. "You talked to them?"

"I did, just as we discussed."

Zara thought it might be best if I met with the king and queen first, and explained her situation. I didn't think they would care, but Zara was insistent that they know what to expect when they meet her. And, I think, she didn't want to be the one to broach the subject of her previous career and who had raised her first.

But I was right. Laurel and Turin don't care. I don't think they could have cared any less. I'd had to repeat myself twice to be sure they'd heard the word *assassin*.

Zara nods.

There's much left to be told—I gave the barest details—but there will be time for that.

"Let's go," she says, squaring her shoulders.

I offer her my hand, and she takes it. Takes it like that's where it belongs, and my heart nearly bursts.

Nina latches onto my other one.

"I need help too," she says, jokingly stroking my arm.

"I'd be happy to help," I say, giving her a tug to bring her flush against my side, and slinging my arm around her.

Nina squeals and pushes me away. "Never mind!"

I laugh, giving Zara's hand a squeeze as we emerge onto the streets of Frigarth.

We arrived a week ago, and we took it all in Zara's own time.

"Did they say anything about the kids?" Zara murmurs, her eyes already stuck on the palace.

"They'll help," I say. "They have rooms in the palace for now, but they'll be placed with families. They'll do all they can to find their real homes, but they'll have a home either way."

She only nods, but a burden seems to have lifted from her shoulders.

I took the two children we'd saved from the assassin compound with me to the palace this morning, explained their situation, and asked for help. Laurel and Turin were more than happy to help of course, and it gave me a good lead in to introduce the topic of having found their daughter too.

It takes us five minutes to walk across to the palace. Zara didn't want to be far, even if she wasn't ready to go until now.

Her hand drifts to her scarf, runs the fabric between her fingers. I don't say anything, don't ask whether she wants to leave it on or take it off. The scar beneath is horrifying, though it is merely a thin silver line. The very thought of the Cutting sends my blood boiling.

Her body is littered with scars that appear nastier, left to their own devices to heal, starting with the fresh one forming on her abdomen. It took nearly two weeks for the tenderness to vanish—nearly the whole walk here from the Kilduin, our pace slowed by her injury. Even now, sometimes I can tell it twinges.

I don't think she'd like to know that I can tell. But she's gotten easier to read as our time together lengthens.

We take the step, Nina gasping at the water passing under our feet, and just like that, we're inside the palace.

"Where are they?" Zara whispers, her voice wobbling.

"Just up here." I stop with her, gesturing to the right, where their figures are hidden by the rows of pillars near the end of the hall.

Zara takes one deep breath, squares her shoulders, and leads the way.

Nina follows close behind me, her face closed off and eyes darting. But I can feel the excitement radiating off her.

Two assassins raised to destroy Frigarth, walking through the palace halls to meet the king and queen.

My smile widens.

Zara rounds the pillars, and a sob echoes from the other side of the attached room.

Laurel and Turin race towards us, and I see Zara's shoulders flex, her hand tightens in mine, but she doesn't move. Doesn't flinch, as her parents come to an almost abrupt halt in front of her. Laurel's arms ache to hold her—it's plain across her face—and one of Turin's own is wrapped around his wife as though to stop himself from diving on his daughter.

My eyes water at the sight, but no one notices as the moment I've dreamed of for seventeen years plays out.

Zara merely stares at them both for a long, long moment, her eyes zipping between them, over them, as though fighting to remember even an inch of them. Her memories are still foggy, and we're not sure how many she'll have. She was only an infant when she was taken.

Finally, Zara turns to Turin, and says, "Would you say something, please?"

His brow crinkles in confusion, but he rumbles, "It's good to see you."

She turns to Laurel expectantly.

My queen smiles through her tears. "Do you prefer Eilah or Zara?"

Zara's hand goes so tight on mine that it hurts.

Finally, she nods. Nods as though she's decided something. Remembered something.

"Zara," she croaks. "It's Zara."

"May we—can we—" Laurel stutters, her hands reaching for Zara.

Zara glances back at me as though making sure I'm still here, though our hands are still glued together.

"Um, OK. Yes."

Laurel and Turin positively dive on her, and I'm pulled along with Zara because her hand doesn't let go. An anchor. I'll be whatever she needs. Whenever she needs it. Eternally, I hope.

The embrace could go on forever, except that Zara begins to wriggle ever so slightly. Prolonged contact. She hates it.

Laurel and Turin awkwardly step back.

Zara clears her throat. "This is my sister Nina."

If they're surprised, it doesn't show on their faces. In fact, it's joy that lights Laurel's eyes as she turns to gaze at the younger girl. Her hand reaches out, and she yanks Nina into her arms.

"You're welcome here as long as you like. You can stay forever if you want."

My queen inviting not one, not two, but four assassins to live in her home. I don't think I could be any happier, any prouder in this moment.

Turin pats Nina's shoulder, his large hand making the small girl appear tiny. But she doesn't seem entirely upset by the adoption that appears to be taking place.

"Would you come for some tea?" Laurel says, "all of you?"

I don't miss the way her eyes linger on my hand still clutched in her daughter's. Their sparkle doubles.

"Yes," Zara says, "I'd like that."

Thank you for coming on this journey with Zara and Raiden! If you'd like to know what happened with the Dragon Assassin, Princess Cyra, and Prince Gaara, check out my free Swan Princess retelling!

Blurb:

Before she was the Fairy Godmother, she was the Swan Princess. Bubbly Princess Cyra is being sent to a neighbouring country to prepare the way for her brother, the king. She's not to talk about the differences between their countries, and especially not about their disagreement on human slavery. But Cyra has a bone to pick with the grumpy Prince Gaara, who called her out on her 'ignorant' behaviour on her last visit. How dare he be so right. She has three goals for this trip.

1. Make Gaara smile.
2. Hold one entire conversation with him.
3. Make him see that she's changed.
And, OK,
4. See if that spark is still there.
But Cyra never makes it there. Kidnapped and trapped in her shifted form, Cyra is left behind as a swan while her attacker takes her place. A deadly plot begins to unfold. And no one suspects a thing. Except Gaara.

Of Swans and Princes is available through my newsletter. Get it here: www.linktr.ee/tianidavids

Pronunciation guide

Names:
    Aeris: Air-ris
    Darius: Dah-ree-us
    Eilah: Eye-la
    Jorai: Joor (like door)- I
    Laurel: Loh-rel
    Nina: Knee-nah
    Raiden: Ray-den
    Turin: Ture-inn
    Zara: Z-are-uh

Locations:
    Ashennor: Ashen-noor
    Dinas Carden: Din-uh-s Car-den
    Ellcombe: El-comb
    Frigarth: Free-garth
    Hythemore: High-th-more
    Kilduin: Kill-due-in

Acknowledgements

Thank you so much for coming on this wild ride with me! Eilah was such a clear character in my mind and to have her realised has been a joy. Raiden, of course, was fantastic to bring back and explore. Putting these two together was magic.

I, of course, have to thank my lovely beta readers once again. Beba, Caroline, and Randi, I love you to the moon and back. Your feedback, your joy, has been invaluable in helping this book come together.

A massive thanks to EJL Editing and the amazing edits I received! You went above and beyond!

Thank you, thank you, thank you to Moorbooks once again for another stunning cover. Seeing this book next to Of Glass and Cinders is a dream come true.

Jesus, my friend and inspiration, thank you.

And thank *you*! Thank you for reading, for your comments, dms, likes and shares. You make this little author's day with every interaction.

Tiani Davids grew up in Victoria reading middle-grade and young adult fantasy, a love that soon expanded to include writing. She now lives on the Far South Coast of New South Wales where she cultivates her passion for reading, writing, and all things Tolkien.

Connect with Tiani:

Instagram: @tianidavids

Facebook: @authortianidavids